LET MY PEOPLE GO

A Glimpse into to the History of Christian Community
in Chamarajanagara Villages, Karnataka (1908-1947)

&

Present Challenges

Includes an account on the life and work of legendary Wesleyan missionary
REV. GEORGE WILLIAM SAWDAY

LET MY PEOPLE GO

A Glimpse into to the History of Christian Community
in Chamarajanagara Villages, Karnataka (1908-1947)

&

Present Challenges

Includes an account on the life and work of legendary Wesleyan missionary
REV. GEORGE WILLIAM SAWDAY

Godwin Shiri

2019

LET MY PEOPLE GO – Published by the Rev. Dr. Ashish Amos of the Indian Society for Promoting Christian Knowledge (ISPCK), Post Box 1585, Kashmere Gate, Delhi-110006.

ISBN: 978-93-88945-14-1

Laser typeset by

ISPCK, Post Box 1585, 1654, Madarsa Road, Kashmere Gate, Delhi-110006 • *Tel:* 23866323

e-mail: ashish@ispck.org.in • ella@ispck.org.in
website: www.ispck.org.in

To my wife

NORA

Companion in life, in days better or worse

Contents

PART - B

Foreword

It was a delight to go through the manuscript of the proposed book of Rev. Dr. Godwin Shiri "Let My People Go..." since it is related to the history and the present condition of village congregations in Chamarajanagara in my Diocese. It is appreciated for highlighting the present challenges of the church in the backdrop of the historical legacy in a region which is still socially and economically backward, mainly due to scarcity of rain. Besides, the inclusion of Rev. G. W. Sawday, a Wesleyan missionary who sowed the seeds of gospel, in the book will be an inspiration for the present generation of Church ministers, especially those working in Chamarajanagara area.

Dr. Godwin Shiri has deep insights on socio-economic concerns of the church in villages and in remote areas. I hope that this book will inspire the present generation, especially Chamarajanagara Christians, to turn their eyes towards the needs of rural churches including Chamarajanagara village congregations.

I heartily congratulate Rev. Dr. Godwin Shiri and wish that more of his thoughts would be seen in the form of writing like this even in the days to come.

Rt. Rev. Mohan Manoraj
Bishop, Karnataka Southern Diocese, CSI
Mangalore

Author's Note

This book is a tribute to the memory of legendary Wesleyan missionary Rev. George William Sawday (1854-1944) and his associates, who toiled and planted churches in Chamarajanagaara (CN) villages, during the first half of last century. The writer does not claim that this writing is all inclusive of the pioneer work they had done, but far from it, he submits that this is only a "glimpse" into their great work.

It has been my long-cherished wish to study Christian community in CN area. I am happy that my wish was finally being realized, by God's Grace, with the active support of many friends and well wishers. Needless to say, the 2-3 years of study was a challenging and learning experience for me, as well as a spiritual experience.

The year 2021 is the Bi-centenary year of the arrival of Wesleyan missionaries to Mysore province. This means we are on the threshhold of a historic event, which should become a time of thanks giving, celebration and re-dedication. It is my earnest hope that this book will serve as a "preparatio" for that historic Bi- centenary event and help in the rejuvenation of our churches, especially in CN area.

I owe a great debt of gratitude to several friends and well wishers for their valuable support which helped in completing the study for this book:

Rev. Dr. Eberhard Will, till recently General Secretary, Ausbildungshilfe-Christian Education Fund, Kassel, Germany, for encouraging me to take up the study. It was on the recommendation of Dr. Will, the EMS, Stuttgart, which supported me with a timely grant to meet the field study expenses. I thank EMS cordially.

Rt. Rev. Mohan Manoraj, Bishop of CSI Karnataka Southern Diocese for encouraging me and supporting this study project, right from the beginning. I also thank him for writing the 'Foreword' to this book.

I am grateful to the Principal of KTC, Mangalore and the Faculty for extending their support, especially in the field study.

Eleven BD III year students, as part of their Practical Work, had done an excellent work of data collection in 26 villages of CN area in October 2016. I thank each of them very cordially for their invaluable assistance.

Rev. Hemachandra, the Area Chairperson and all the Presbyters and lay leaders of CN area for extending an ungrudging support.

I owe a great debt of gratitude to the pastors, Rev. Thyagaraj and Rev. Usha Thyagaraj based in Chamarajanagara town. Both had extended a very warm hospitality whenever I visited CN area and had given an invaluable support to this study. In fact, Rev. Thyagaraj was my very trusted 'guide' to the CN village congregations during the entire course of the study.

I am thankful to the archivist of UT College library, Bengaluru and to Mr. Benet Amanna, archivist of KTC library for their kind co-operation and support while collecting the primary resources.

Rev. Dr. H.M. Watson, Professor of Systematic Theology, KTC, Mangalore, has contributed an 'Introduction' to this volume. Coming from a young scholar of commitment and in-depth knowledge and perception of grass root situation, his introduction has enriched the value of this book. I thank him very cordially.

I am grateful to my wife Nora, for doing all the typing and secretarial work and meticulously preparing the final manuscript for publication. I am indebted for her labour of love.

The astounding work done by Sawday and his associates in CN area is indeed greatly inspiring, for all times. The remarkably committed and liberative work which they had accomplished in leading an oppressed people in its 'exodus' is exemplary and inspiring, even for today.

True, CN churches have a glorious past. However, under the constant pressure of a multiple factor which includes recurring failure of rain, rapidly turning unproductive agriculture, lack of job opportunities, escalation of migration and a gradual weakening or collapse of pastoral care appear to have pushed the Christian community into a situation which is inexplicably deplorable. Once pulsating with so much of life and hope, now the condition of village congregation is fast turning to be like that of a 'withered tree'! The findings of the Sample survey which was conducted as part of this study clearly unravel the depressing situation.

It is time, and it is an urgent 'Macedonian Call' that the church leadership as well as all those who are genuinely concerned about the growth and witness of the church in CN area and elsewhere should wake up to rejuvenate the congregations.

Godwin Shiri
Bengaluru

Introduction

Chamarajanagar has attached a negative tag to its name. The reason behind it is not known to anybody, but it has resulted in superstition and affected the people living in Chamarajanagar. However some people have tried to break it. It is believed that if a political leader visits Chamarajanagar he/she loses his/her position. Because of this belief many political leaders avoided visiting this region. However Sri Siddaramaya, a leader with the zeal for social justice tried to break the ice. He visited the area and proved the belief wrong; he completed his tenure as a successful chief minister of Karnataka. Such biased opinion and attitude is an exception to religious matters. Among Christians too one could see it. The Christian community of this region has been marginalized because of such attitude towards them by Christians from other area. However, through his work entitled *Let My People Go: A Glimpse into to the History of Christian Community in Chamarajanagara Villages, Karnataka (1908-1947)*, Dr. Godwin Shiri, a theologian with commitment and conviction of social justice seems to bring justice to the marginalized Christian community of Chamarajanagar. Not much work has been done in relation to the Wesleyan missionary work in Chamarajanagar area. Though Christians from this area have contributed a lot in the life and growth of churches and institutions in Mysore and

Bangalore, not much study or research is done on this region. In this context Dr. Shiri's work should be recognised, appreciated and supported.

The book has two parts: Part A consists of 10 chapters and these chapters include mainly the descriptive narrations of the missionary work in the particular context. Though the focus of the book is the work of Wesleyan mission in Chamarajanagar, related descriptions help one to have a better understanding on the subject. A detailed portrayal of Chamarajanagar helps one to get a general picture of the area in which missionary work took place. On the other hand, an account of the general work of the Wesleyan mission facilitates to locate the mission work in Chamarajanagar. Chapters 3 to 8 deal mainly with the work of the Mission in Chamarajanagar and with the Christian communities in different parts of that area. The presented narration not only depicts a historical bird-view of the missionary work and their zeal but also illustrates Dr. Shiri's passion for the social justice and his concern for the downtrodden people. Sometimes, due to the positive and passionate language which he uses in his narration of incidents, one tends to assume that the author's presentation is too subjective; however we should remember that the author does not belong to this church tradition (Wesleyan) and does not come from this region. Hence it only indicates his inclination towards social justice which becomes clear in his own statement. He says, "The remarkably committed and liberative work which they had accomplished in leading an oppressed people in its 'exodus' is exemplary and inspiring for even today." Chapter 9 deals with the life and work of the legendary Wesleyan missionary Sawday which is well suited to the book as the Wesleyan mission work in Mysore and Chamarajanagar, which otherwise cannot be understood without knowing Sawday.

Part B of the book deals with the present socio-economic conditions of Christians in Chamarajanagar. This is the outcome of Dr. Shiri's empirical field study. Dr. Shiri is known for his expertise in field studies and it is evident in this book too.

Dr. Shiri's book provides ample materials for further research and systematic analysis of the missionary work in Chamarajanagar area. Though the author has not much involved in critical analysis and evaluation, his introductory remarks indicate that his book is not without these aspects. He has rightly said, "True, CN churches have a glorious past.   However, under the constant pressure of a multiple factor which includes recurring failure of rain, agriculture rapidly turning unproductive, lack of job opportunities, escalation of migration and a gradual weakening or collapse of pastoral care appear to have resulted in a situation which is inexplicably deplorable.   Once pulsating with so much of life and hope, now the condition of village congregations is fast turning to be like that of a 'withered tree'! The findings of the Sample survey which was conducted as part of this study clearly unravel the depressing situation." His call for "the Church leadership as well as all those who are genuinely concerned about the growth and witness of the Church in CN area and elsewhere ... (to) wake up and act which would go a long way in rejuvenating the congregations" has come out aptly with a challenge for us now. It should be noted that most of the pastors from Wesleyan Methodist background are from Chamrajanagar area. There are clouds of leaders in the secular field who live in Mysore and Bangalore, and they hail from Chamrajanagar. The present bishop of CSI Karnataka Southern Diocese is from the same Chamrajanagar area. But why the common people who live in Chamrajanagar are still in pathetic condition? This is an important question one needs to ponder upon. Hence, Dr. Shiri's observation and call should serve as a challenge when the Bi-centenary year of arrival of Wesleyan missionaries to Mysore province is only few years ahead from now.

My best wishes to Dr. Godwin Shiri for his book and I wish and pray that the book will enlighten, inspire and challenge not only Christians from Chamarajanagar but also all the faithful followers of our Lord and Saviour Jesus Christ elsewhere.

Rev. Dr. H.M. Watson,
Professor, Systematic Theology,
Karnataka Theological College, Mangalore

PART - A

CHAPTER - 1

Chamarajanagara District

General background

Chamarajanagara is a district in Karnataka state located in the southernmost tip of the state. It is situated 175 kilometers south of state capital, Bengaluru and 70 kilometers south east of Mysore city, the cultural capital of Karnataka. Chamarajanagara was a part of the erstwhile Mysore district as a taluk for a long time. However, in 1997 this taluk was made as a separate district with Chamarajanagara town as the headquarters of the newly formed district. Presently, this district has five taluks which include Chamarajanagara, Gundlupet, Yallandur, Hanur and Kollegal.

Geographical

The geographical location of Chamarajanagara (hereafter CN) district, located at the southernmost tip of the Karnataka, is very striking:

On the *east and the south,* the picturesque Biligiri Rangana Hills (BR Hills) provide a natural border with the neighboring Tamil Nadu state. In fact, CN district looks like a vast valley of lush green BR Hills.

On the *north* the historic temple town T. Narasipur is located. This place is a *sangama* or confluence of three rivers namely Cauvery, Kabini and Spatika.

On the *western* side the district is adjacent to famous temple town Nanjanagud which is half way between Mysore city and CN town.

On the *south west* of the district Gundlupet town/taluk, which touches the picturesque Nilagiri Hill ranges of Tamil Nadu, is located. Bandipur National Sanctuary is in Gundlupet taluk. Part of the south western border touches Wayanad of Kerala state.

Thus, the geographical setting of CN district is very picturesque. Surrounded with BR Hills, Male Mahadeshwara Hill, waterfalls of Shivana Samudra, ranges of sandalwood forests in eastern borders, Bandipur Sanctuary and so on the CN district really looks idyllic.

The great triangle

Missionary reports of early last century have often described the 'Nanajanagud-Chamarajanagara town –Gundlupet-Nanjanagud' route as a fascinating triangle with each of the side twenty-five miles long. Tomlinson called it as 'the great triangle' (Sargant, p 41). The Wesleyan missionaries used to travel from Mysore city to Nanjanagud by train, overnight in that temple town, and then proceed further to the CN villages, by bullock carts. The 35 kilometers Nanjanagud-CN town stretch used to take about ten hours by bullock cart in those days! When the Mysore-Nanjanagud railway line was extended up to CN town in 1926 that became a boon to the region.

Once a green forest area- now a vast dry area

CN villages which are spread out like a valley of B.R. Hills on the south and eastern side were once said to be filled with green forests, in habited by tribal people namely, Soligas. However, over the centuries the area was believed to have become a 'hideout' for those runaway people who wanted to escape from the killings and the rampage by war lords and marauding enemy soldiers as well as atrocities of upper castes. Eventually, the runaway people settled down in CN area, built hamlets and started cultivation. As the waves of refugees steadily increased the landscape of the area began to change. With the cultivation activities increasing forests disappeared and rainfall became scantier. With the passing of time the original inhabitants, Adivasis retreated into thicker forests of BR Hills.

In the meanwhile, with the continued influx of people from outside many villages sprang up in CN area and a caste-ruled society began to take deeper roots.

'Arikotara' becomes Chamarajanagara

It is interesting that until early 19th century CN town was known as 'Arikotara'! The word 'Arikotara' most likely meant 'abode of elephant herds', pointing out to a time how the area was once filled with forests and wild life. When the then Maharaja of Mysore Mummadi Krishanaraja Wodeyar (1799-1831)during one of his hunting trips to the area came to know that his father Khasa Chamaraja Wodeyar (1776-1796) was born in Arikotara he re-christened it as 'Chamarajanagara' to perpetuate his father's memory. Thus from 1818 Arikotara became Chamarajanagara (MDR 1886, p.28). The Mysore king also built a big temple in 1828 and a palace there. While the temple remains a landmark at the centre of the town, the palace was however ruined due to misconstruction. From that time CN began to grow fast as a commercial and administrative centre for the entire area. Later, CN town had also served as a taluk headquarters, within Mysore district.

In 1997 when this taluk became a full pledged CN district the CN town became the district headquarters.

Cultivation- mostly dependent on rain water

It is striking, that a larger part of a land which is surrounded with long hill ranges with lush green forests like BR Hills and Nilgiris should be dry one! Obviously deforestation which has been taking place over the centuries is one main reason for this situation. Under this circumstance agriculture in most of CN area is totally dependent on unpredictable and scant rainfall. There are a few small tributaries of Cauvery such as Honnuhole or Survarnavathi, Nugu, Chikkahole and so on but those rivers are too small ones. Besides they remain dried up during most time of the year! Obviously, there are several small streams and ponds in the area, but they are filled with some water only when it rains. Wells and bore wells have been dug up in large numbers, all over. However, since the underground water has greatly depleted with the passing of the years, bore wells are either totally dried up or yield little or no water.

Drinking water becomes a great scarcity in CN villages, especially during summer season. Needless to state that along with people live stock also undergo a miserable time without water, during the recurring dry spells in the district.

As per recent reports the average rain fall in the district is a mere 751mm, which is far below state average of 1248 mm (compare with Udupi district average- 4119mm, and Dakshina Kannada district 3975 mm). At times there is absolutely no rain fall continuously for two years or even more, making the living condition of people and the livestock inexplicably miserable. People stare at sky for rainfall, expectantly and endlessly, day in and day out, but in vain. People frantically search for coolie work; however, it is very difficult to get even a coolie work during drought periods. It is at this time usually people's migration escalates. In fact, this is the usual 'story' of CN area, since time unknown.

When it rains people cultivate jholam (maize), ragi, millets and vegetables. In a few parts of the district where water resource is relatively better, especially in the eastern part of the district, people cultivate paddy, sugar cane and mulberry and so on. At one stage mulberry cultivation and silk yarn making were flourishing in the area. Kollegal town was a noted centre for silk industry. However, since last few decades silk industry in the district is almost on the total decline.

CN – a district with rapid migration

In a situation where agriculture was becoming increasingly unproductive and other employment opportunities were scarce people appear to be having little or no choice but to migrate to other places for survival. The social/caste oppression which was suffocating the mass also greatly added to the 'push out' process or migration of people from villages to outside places.

The historic records of the 19th century, including the missionary journals point out how people used to migrate from CN villages to other places, even to overseas, in search of livelihood. It is interesting that as far back as 2-3 centuries people of this region had migrated to coffee/ tea estates of Nilgiris, Wayanad, Coorg and even to the distant Ceylon (Sri Lanka). At a time, proper housing, sanitation and medical care were either totally lacking or in a very primitive condition, countless people were migrating to those distant estates for their livelihood. While many died on the way itself, a large number used to die while living and working in very hostile and unhealthy living conditions of the estates. True, some among the migrant labourers who survived all the hardships could improve their living condition to an extent and were able to give some support to their families back home in CN villages.

From early 20th century a new pattern of migration began to develop. Thousands of people from CN villages, instead to coffee/tea estates, began migrating to places within Karnataka where industries were fast developing. They also began to migrate to areas where agriculture had begun to flourish due to construction of huge water reservoirs. Thus, people from CN villages started migrating to Mysore, Mandya, industrial towns like Bhadravathi and few other places beyond the state. Finally, the fast-growing Bengaluru, capital of Karnataka became the most favored destination of countless number of migrants! Bengaluru, with ample opportunities for labour, especially in the unorganized sector, started beckoning and 'pulling in' ever growing number of migrants from all over, including from CN villages.

CN—a district with a tag as 'inauspicious'

In a situation where, agricultural activities had a very limited scope due to scarce/erratic rain fall, hardly any industries worth mentioning developed in the area. A general, nay a chronic socio-economic backwardness continued to linger in the area, without any noticeable change or progress at all.

Not only with regard to socio-economic growth or employment, even in literacy and educational prospects CN district has perennially lagged behind. With 61.43% literacy, CN district is the third district in the state with lowest literacy level.

Critics charge that the apathy of the government was one main reason behind the chronic underdeveloped condition of the district. The district of course is well endowed with rich resources including mineral resources such as chromate, graphite and magnesium etc., but the benefit of those resources does not seem to be helping the development of the area/people, anyway. It is often complained that the political leaders have been apathic towards the needs of the people. Further it is often said that the State leaders are very fearful/apprehensive to visit the district because of a long nurtured superstitious belief that they might lose their 'seat of power' if they step into this district, since it is a bad omen!

Demographic facts

In ancient times subaltern customs and traditions used to be ruling the socio-political institutions of the people in CN hamlets. However, with the influx of people from outside the social ethos of the area had steadily changed. The runaway people who flooded into CN terrain brought along with them their social order especially caste culture to the new place. The society which eventually evolved was divisive and hierarchical with people belonging to different demarcated castes, upper, lower and outcastes. Obviously, untouchability and caste oppression took deeper roots and became accepted social norm. Illiteracy, ignorance and superstition which were inexplicably rampant among people provided a fertile ground to caste system to grow and flourish, with all its evils and aberrations. Further, the caste ideology stunted the very social progress of people.

Understandably the depressed class, backward classes, women and subaltern people became the worst victims in that emerging social milieu.

People's groups in CN district

Today Lingayats, Brahmins, numerous Shudra communities, Dalits, Scheduled tribes, Muslims, Christians are the main people's groups living in CN district. The people belonging to Shudra communities are the most numerous in the district.

Lingayatism entered CN region around three hundred years ago making a strong appeal and winning a large number from Shudra communities. Over the passing of time the enterprising Lingayats have become a landed people and a dominant community. Today Lingayats are the most dominant community, socio-economically and politically in CN area.

Brahmins, though small, due to their historically privileged socio-religious status, are in a dominant position same way as the Lingayats.

Among the Shudra communities include, Kuruba, Parivara, Naik, Kumbara, Ganiga, Naiks, Akkasalaru, Badiga, Madivala, Pujari (Thammadiga), Agasa and several other groups. Some of the Shudra communities hold small pieces of land and are marginal farmers. However, among the weaker Shudra communities the great majority are landless, poor and illiterate. In fact, their condition is very much like that of Dalits, except that they are not treated as untouchables in the villages. In recent few years some of the Shudra communities are developing an increased political consciousness and caste unity among themselves which is considerably helping them to gain some socio-political advantage.

Muslims are found in good number especially in CN town, Kiragsur, Kavalande and in few other villages. Great majority of the Muslims are engaged in petty business. With poverty and illiteracy thriving among most of the Muslims, their living condition is very similar to that of backward class/Shudra communities.

Christians are in a much smaller number in CN district. As per census 2011 they comprised 2.17 percent of the total population of the district. Most of the Christians are thinly populated in about 20-25 villages, mostly in eastern part of the district. Almost all Christians of CN area hail from Holeya community. Like rest of the depressed communities, Holeyas also are a historically oppressed community. The Wesleyan missionaries worked among them during the first half of last century and succeeded in reaching a segment of Holeya population. However, even after conversion their socio-economic condition remains deplorable, due to many reasons especially the historic disadvantages they suffer because of their out caste (SC) origin. More about this subject will be dealt in detail in later chapters.

The CN district has a large number of 'Hindu' Dalit population. As per 2011 census the Dalits comprise a high 25.4 percent of the CN district's total population. This is higher than Karnataka state percentage of Dalits which stands at 17.15 percent as per 2011 census. It may be noted that the CN district has the second highest Dalit population, district wise, in the state.

The Dalits in CN district belong to various out caste communities such as Holeya, Madiga. Chaluvadi and so on. The Holeyas are the majority among the Dalits in the district. As noted earlier CN Christians hail from Holeya origin who embraced Christian faith during the first half of last century when the Wesleyan Mission was active in the area.

It is generally agreed upon that the Dalits are the indigenous people of CN villages. It is contested that they were the first to enter CN area as 'runaway' people and started cultivating land there and settling down. They were cultivators and they owned the land. However, when the subsequent waves of migrants comprising dominant caste people came, the Dalits became landless and eventually reduced to be serfs and slaves of the dominant castes. Even today the condition of Dalits in CN area, as in most parts of the country, continues to be very vulnerable. They are the poorest of the poor and continue to be in the lowest strata of the society from every index of human development.

The district has 11.8% of people belonging to Scheduled Tribe (ST) category. The ST communities in the district include, Soliga, Jenu Kuruba, Kadu Kuruba, Lambani and so on. The living condition of STs is very similar to Dalits and Shudras. They live steeped deep in poverty and illiteracy, with hardly any noticeable change in their living condition.

Few Basic Data of CN district

1.	Total population	1,020.721
2.	Total area	5,648km
3.	Density	181 per sq km
4.	Urban population	17.14%
5.	Rural population	82.86%
6.	Literacy	61.43% (State: 75.36%)
		Male literacy-67.93% Female-54.92%
7.	Sex ratio	1000-993
8.	Religion	Hindu-92.29%, Muslim-4.62%, Christian-2.17%
9.	SC population	25.4% (State-17.15%)
10.	ST population	11.8% (State-6.95%)
11.	Average rainfall	751 mm

(Source: 2011 Census Report)

Political

CN area was under the control of warring feudal lords or 'palegars' though the region was part of different rulers like Ganga, Chalukya, Chola, Hoysala, Vijayanagara, Wodeyars and so on, at different times. Palegars fought between themselves, endlessly, and therefore killing spree, lootings, pillage and rampage were common occurrences. The small town Ummathur in present CN taluk was said to be palegars' capital for a long time. There existed hardly any semblance of peace or stability in the land. Further in a land where caste had taken deeper roots, the lower caste people particularly the Dalits were treated in very harsh ways.

From around 16th century the region came under the rule of Mysore kings, Wodeyars. Even then, the local control of palegars continued for quite a long time giving little or no chance for any significant development taking place or peace to prevail in the area.

Finally, when the British defeated Tippu Sultan in 1799 the entire Mysore province along with CN area came under the overall supremacy of British rulers, while the Wodeyars continued as the subordinate administrators. This heralded a new era, with some radical changes in the administration. CN area was made as a taluk of the erstwhile Mysore district, an administrative arrangement which continued for a long period. It was in 1997 the Karnataka state government declared CN taluk as a full-pledged district and thus facilitated a new era in the history of the region with the promise of progress in the area.

CHAPTER – 2

Arrival of Wesleyan Missionaries in Mysore Province

The rise and growth of pietism in Germany and the Methodist movement in England in 18th and 19th centuries were phenomenal development in the history of Christianity in Europe. Those pietistic/evangelical movements had far reaching influence on the life and the witness of the church. While on the one hand the pietistic movement made personal piety and holiness of all believers as very basic to Christian life, on the other it underlined the global proclamation of the Gospel or evangelization as an imperative duty of all Believers. These two basics were the hallmark of pietistic/evangelical movements which started stirring up a renewal within the churches in Europe. As a result, a number of missionary societies were established, one after another, in 18th and 19thcenturies and the missionaries were sent, far and wide.

Interestingly that was also the time when the Western powers were busy engaged in bitter fights to establish their colonies or political power all over the world, vying with each other for supremacy!

The Methodist church was an outstanding fruit of pietistic/ evangelical movement in England, founded during the last quarter of 18th century, creating great ripples of renewal within the Church in England. Within a few years the Methodist church began sending missionaries to many countries. However, the long-felt dream of the Methodist church to send missionaries to India was not realized for long. Finally, in 1813, when the British Parliament constitutionally approved Christian Mission work in colonial India, the doors for the Methodist Mission work were opened.

Arrival of Wesleyan Methodist missionaries to Mysore province

Dr. Thomas Coke and his initiatives to establish Wesleyan Mission work in India

Dr Thomas Coke acclaimed as the 'Pioneer of Wesleyan Missions' was a close associate of John Wesley, the founder of Methodist church. Coke was a staunch advocate of evangelization of entire world. He was particularly very keen that the Methodist church sent its missionaries to India. After much lobbying he finally succeeded in convincing the Methodist church authorities to agree to send few missionaries to India. Coke himself contributed a large sum of 6000/ pounds for the purpose.

On December 30, 1813 along with five others, Coke started sailing to India. However, after four months of voyage he died on the way and he was buried in the sea. The rest of the members of the team continued their voyage and managed to reach Ceylon. There they started working with the support of some local based British officers. Although Dr. Coke's lifelong dream to reach India for missionary work was not realized during his life time, the role he played as a forerunner in the eventual establishment of Wesleyan Mission work in India was remarkable.

Increasing pressure on Methodist church to send missionaries to India

In the first quarter of 19th century several direct appeals were received by the Methodist church in England to send missionaries to India. Those appeals further expedited the Methodist church to make a final decision on the matter. In 1816 a group of British officers of Wesleyan background based in Madras also had sent an appeal to Jaffna Synod of the Methodist church to send missionaries to come and work in India.

Further Christian David, a personal attendant of the celebrated Lutheran missionary Schwartz, during his visit to Jaffna greatly aroused interest among the Methodist missionaries working there on the need of working in India. All those pressurized the Methodist church Home Committee to make a final decision to send missionaries to India.

Arrival of first Wesleyan missionaries to Madras in 1817

Under the growing pressure from many quarters the Methodist church in England finally sent its first missionary, Rev. James Lynch to Madras in 1817. He labored mainly among the British soldiers and their native servant class. In 1819 Lynch sent a report to the Home Committee informing that there were facilities for the establishment of a Mission in Bangalore in Mysore country. As a response the Home Committee in 1820 appointed two missionaries Rev. Elijah Hoole and Rev. James Mowat to work in Mysore country. After a turbulent voyage those two first reached Ceylon and then sailed to Madras.

Rev. Elijah Hoole the first Wesleyan Missionary to enter Mysore country in 1821

The year 1821 is historical year for the Wesleyan missionaries work in the Mysore province.

Rev. Hoole travelled in palanquin from Madras to Nagapatnam and from there proceeded to Bangalore. When he reached Bangalore on 29th April 1821, he became the first Wesleyan (Methodist) missionary ever to enter Mysore country. The second Wesleyan missionary Rev. Mowat reached Bangalore in June 1821 along with his wife.

Both Hoole and Mowat began their work among the British and the Tamil working class in Bangalore. In July 1821 Hoole along with the Madras based Wesleyan missionary Titus Close visited Srirangapatna and Mysore city on an inspection visit. They found a small church in Srirangapatna where a small group of British and Tamil Christians was gathering for worship. It was during this visit the young Hoole met the noted Catholic missionary old Abbe Dubois in the fort of Srirangapatna.

Although both Hoole and Mowat started working, intensively, especially among the British and the Tamils, they could not continue in Bangalore for a long time. Due to some unforeseen emergency arising in Madras area both the missionaries were transferred from Bangalore in 1824. Hoole left Bangalore reluctantly. The Wesleyan Mission work which began in Mysore province in 1821 was thus almost disbanded in 1824 due to the unexpected transfers of the missionaries, Hoole and Mowat.

Although the Wesleyan missionaries started working in Mysore province from 1821 the work was almost exclusively confined to Bangalore. Moreover the work was mostly confined among the British soldiers and Tamil working class. Further, as noted earlier, the work had suffered great deal of setback due to unforeseen transfers of the first two missionaries, Hoole and Mowat. It was only after about 15 years namely from around mid 1830s the work was picked up again, with some intensity. (E. W. Thompson,

The Call of India, WMMS, London, 1912; MDR, 1921, One
Hundred Years of Wesleyan Mission, et al).

Political transition in Mysore province

In 1830s while the Mission work was beginning to intensify the
Mysore province was undergoing some important political changes.
After the defeat of Tippu Sultan in 1799 the British rulers had
reinstated Wodeyars in royal throne. However, after about three
decades of Wodeyar rule the British rulers began to feel that the
political disturbances and instability were on the increase for which
they thought that some unwise decisions of Maharaja were the
reason. Under this circumstance in 1831 they made a final decision
and appointed a British Resident Commissioner to administer
the entire province, directly. According to the new arrangement
Mysore Maharaja became a nominal head. Many thought that the
direct British rule was good for the greater stability and order in
the province and would expedite progress of people. The Wesleyan
missionaries too believed that the transition namely the direct
rule of British over Mysore province through a British Resident
Commissioner could be beneficial, especially to their Mission
work. Therefore, they welcomed the political transition of 1831.

Missionaries' expectation was realized in quite many ways.
Many godly British officers in the administration helped the
Mission in several ways, especially in giving some indirect
protection as well as in acquiring lands and sites for the Mission
work.

After about half a century namely in 1881 the British rulers
reinstated Wodeyars once again as the rulers of Mysore province
under the supreme authority of British Crown. As far as the
missionaries were concerned initially, they carried some anxiety
about this transition of power (MDR, 1880, p.3). However,

the Wodeyars proved to be enlightened and progressive rulers, exemplary among all the princes of native states (Findley and Holdsworth, pp.288-89). Wesleyan missionaries carried high respect towards Wodeyars and maintained a cordial relationship with them. Missionaries reported that the Mysore Maharajah though'an orthodox Hindu but genuinely concerned for the progress of the people, an upright ruler held in respect by the subjects' (MDR, 1934, p.66).

Enter Rev. Thomas Hodson- "Father of Mysore Mission" - 1833

In 1833 the Wesleyan Mission transferred Rev. Thomas Hodson to Bangalore who was until then working in Calcutta. Although he was sent to Bangalore to work among the English and Tamils it is very striking that eventually he turned out to be the pioneer Wesleyan missionary to work among Kannada people. How that was transpired was an interesting story:

Almost coinciding with the arrival of Hodson there was a growing feeling in the Mission circle that the work among Kannada people should be taken up more seriously. As indicated earlier, although the Mission started working in the Mysore province from 1821 almost all the native Christians as well as all native ministers and catechists were Tamils. The Missionary authorities began to see that the absence of Kannada work was a serious lapse and strongly felt the urgent need of working among the Kannada people. Incidentally in 1834 a letter from Home Committee also recommended that instead of working among English and Tamils, the work of the Mission may focus on Kannada people. As a follow up to this suggestion, an appeal was sent from India to the Home Committee to send four men to work exclusively among Kannada people. At this time of major policy change

Hodson had to bear a great responsibility on his shoulders and he discharged it with utmost commitment and wisdom.

Hodson establishes first Wesleyan Mission station in Gubbi -1837

As the realization about the need of concentrating Mission work more among Kannada people greatly increased, Hodson who was then based in Bangalore embarked on an exploratory trip of the land with an objective to open Mission stations. In 1836 he went to Mysore, from there to Coorg and then to West Coast and returned to Bangalore via Tumkur. While he was in Tumkur he took a horse ride to the neighboring small town of Gubbi. When he rode into Gubbi town people lined up in great excitement, welcoming him, mistaking him to be the well-known Major Dobbs, Chief British Officer based in Tumkur. Hodson was accorded much hospitality. However, it did not take much time for the people to realize that the visitor was not Dobbs but a missionary.

During his stay in Gubbi, Hodson concluded that Gubbi could be an ideal place to establish a Mission station. He saw that the town was much free from the Brahminic orthodoxy and on the other hand also free from the unwanted influence of English people (Findley, D.D and Holdsworth, W.W, *History of WMMS,* Volume.V, London,1924 p.275). Besides he also realized that Gubbi was located almost in the centre of erstwhile Mysore province. The Home Committee and the Kanarese section of Madras Council of Wesleyan Mission soon approved Hodson's recommendation and thus from April 1837 the little town of Gubbi became the first Wesleyan Mission station in Mysore province.

Hodson resided in Gubbi along with his wife. John Jenkins was his associate missionary in Gubbi. By 1839 a missionary house, assistant missionary house and a prayer shed were built in Gubbi. It may be noted that those were to be the first ever Wesleyan Mission constructions in entire Mysore province, including Bangalore.

Hodson Opens Mission stations in Mysore, Bangalore and in more places

In 1838 Hodson visited Mysore. At that time Mysore was a city with about 70,000 people. He bought a Bungalow from Mysore Maharaja and laid the foundation of Wesleyan Mission work in and around Mysore city. In the same year he opened Mission stations in Kunigal and Bangalore. In 1839 a Kanarese circuit was constituted within the Wesleyan Madras district to which the Mysore province work belonged up to that time. Starting of a Kanarese circuit gave a much-needed boost to speed up the work among Kannada people. In the same year namely 1839 Hodson built a Bungalow and set up a Mission press in Bangalore.

In 1841 the first ever Wesleyan congregation was formed in Bangalore. That was exclusively a Tamil congregation.

Chikka-the first Kannada convert, Gubbi, 1843

It is interesting that after 22 years since the Wesleyan Mission started work in Mysore province the first Kannada person was baptized in 1843! That person was Chikka, a young washer man of Gubbi. Mathew T. Male, the missionary based in Gubbi gave baptism to Chikka. Chikka became Daniel after baptism (MDR, 1921, *One Hundred Year*, p.36).

Temporary standstill of Mission work in 1851

The work of the Wesleyan Mission unexpectedly came to a standstill in 1851 since funds stopped coming to the Mission work in Mysore province. The staff was retrenched. Mysore station was left without a staff. Gubbi establishment including Mission house and chapel were sold! Work in Gubbi completely closed. It was a crisis. Entire work came to a standstill. The crisis occurred because of the 'protesters' at home, in England (Thompson, p.144). The crisis held up the work for a year. The problems were however cleared after a year and the work was resumed. Due to the crisis it took about four years for the work to resume in Gubbi (Findley and. Holdsworth,… pp. 270-271).

Mission work takes an expansion in Mysore province

After the crisis noted above was over, from late 1850s the Wesleyan Mission work in Mysore province was reactivated and began expanding. Findley and Holdsworth reported how after the Provincial Synod in 1859 the Mission work reactivated: '… but that year(1859) was really the beginning of a new era for the Mission, and from that time its progress was continuous and it marked by the consolidation of every position gained' (Ibid, p.273).

During those days, Mysore province included four cities namely, Bangalore city, Bangalore Cantonment, Mysore city and KGF, and eight districts. The eight districts were: Bangalore, Kolar, Tumkur, Mysore, Chitradurga, Hassan, Kadur and Shimoga.

Besides the first four stations namely Gubbi, Mysore, Bangalore and Kunigal which were established earlier, new ones were opened in Tumkur, Hassan, KGF, Mandya, Chikamagalur, Chitradurga and so on. The number of missionaries arriving to India was also greatly increased. More and more catechists and evangelists were recruited. Schools, boarding homes, orphanages were established in many Mission centres. Bangalore and Mysore became two very prominent centres, where the Wesleyan Mission's work especially in the educational field became pioneering and outstanding.

'While people were generally responsive to the Gospel preaching, in terms of conversions the result was rather disheartening. The missionaries felt that their years of toil did not yield expected result at all. For example, in Mysore city where the Mission work was started in 1838 there were just six full members in 1850. Missionaries carried much frustration about the very dismal number of conversions. They exclaimed 'there is little to hearten much to depress' (MDR. 1850, p.20). They lamented how often their hands hang down and hearts ready to faint and were weary from discouragement (Ibid, 29). After 40 years of work, Mysore city had just 100 members in 1878. The poor result for their decade long labor, especially in terms of number of conversions, remained an enigmatic question to them, about which they worried much and debated for long.

In fact, the slow growth of the church was the general phenomenon not only in Mysore city but almost in the entire Mysore province, where the Wesleyan missionaries were working. As a small consolation or solace Bangalore city and KGF were yielding some encouraging harvest among the Tamils.

The little congregations in Mysore city

In initial two decades the little flocks of Wesleyan Mission in Mysore city included mostly British officials and Tamil servant class. It was from around mid 1850s when tiny congregations begun to be formed in Holagerry and Yerrangerry in Mysore city. Members were locals and people belonged to the bottom class of the society. In 1876 the Wesleyan Mission annual report stated that there were 150 souls in Mysore out of which 73 were communicants. Further it was stated that they belonged to three categories, namely, 1. Gardeners 2. Persons in the lower grade of government employment and 3. domestic servants (MDR, 1876.p.18).

A statement in 1878 clearly reiterates the humble social status of Christian community:" True the members are poor, their influence is scarcely felt at all in the town, they are often spoken of with contempt" (MDR,1878, p.19).

Some important features of Wesleyan Mission work in early period

Proclamation of the Gospel

Wesleyan Mission had always perceived, like most of the Protestant Missions working in India, that proclamation of the Gospel was the primary duty as well as the priority. Proclamation was done mainly through preaching in towns and villages, in places wherever people gather. The preaching of the Gospel always accompanied with the distribution/sale of scripture portions and other Christian literature. People generally listened to missionary preaching with interest. They used to usually marvel to see the way the white-skinned missionaries were preaching in chaste Kannada!

Missionary preaching was generally critical of indigenous religions and culture (MDR, One Hundred Years ....1921, p.24). This used to anger Hindu orthodox people. Missionaries however, tended to think that a critical approach on native religions and culture was essential because it helped to quicken people's conscience towards the rampant abuse of religion manifesting itself in umpteen number of perennial social evils (Ibid). In later decades the missionaries mellowed down in their criticism of Hinduism, considerably.

While the mass generally listened to missionary preaching with interest or with curiosity, this was not the case with Hindu orthodoxy or the people who belonged to upper castes. Right from the beginning orthodox section of the population haunted missionaries by obstructing, harassing and humiliating through every way possible.

Educational work-opening of schools

The missionaries were quick to realize that mere verbal proclamation/preaching would not be sufficient to reach people. It was stated: 'Preaching Christ was the first work of the new missionaries. But no one who has Christ spirit can be content to live among needy men and women and children, and only preach' (Ibid, p.25) . As early as in 1838 they had stated: 'To save the souls of those to whom we have been sent is indeed the ultimate object ever kept in every department of labour in which we have been engaged. But in the pursuit of this object other very important, but incidental, benefits have been imparted' (MDR,1848, p.31). The missionaries conceded that some time those incidental things were more appreciated than those spiritual.

Establishment of schools was the first and foremost task they undertook.. Missionaries saw rampant illiteracy everywhere on the one hand and the resultant ignorance/superstition on the other. Since missionaries believed that the ignorance is a great obstacle, it was thought that, its removal through educational work may help people to receive Gospel (ibid). It should also be noted that they noticed much desire or motivation among people for education especially English education. The government was also very appreciative and supportive of the educational work of Mission. All these greatly encouraged the missionaries to venture into educational work more intensively (Thompson, p.141).

The educational work done by the Wesleyan Mission was remarkable and it greatly helped to usher in a new era of enlightenment in the land. It is too vast to make a list of schools the Wesleyan Mission had established in different parts of the

Mysore province and it is beyond the scope of the present study also.

Wesleyan Mission- pioneer of female education

It is a universally known fact that Indian women were deprived of education from time unknown. However, from the beginning of 19th century under the British administration a change began to take place and women slowly found access to educational institutions. It was very revealing that the Christian Missions all over the country remarkably helped to this catalytic change. This is very much true of Wesleyan Mission also working in Mysore province. The Wesleyan Mission started schools and boarding schools exclusively meant for female students. As early as in 1844 they started a Girls boarding home in Mysore (One Hundred... p29). Schools exclusively for girls were also started. The combined effect of all those efforts was far reaching and remarkably catalytic. The statistics speak to themselves:

In 1850 out of 148 students studying in four Mission schools in Mysore city there was not even a single female student! In fact, this was the case in most of the schools in entire Mysore province. However, with the surge for female education rapidly growing by the turn of 19th century there were literally hundreds of female students in schools, including in Wesleyan Mission schools. Findley and Holdsworth stated that in 1850 there were only 15 girls in Mission schools in entire province, in 1859 there were eighty and in 1869 there were 580 girls (Findley and Holdsworth.... p. 279). The female numbers in schools went on escalating, unabated, from 1850s.

Wesleyan Mission played a pioneering and pivotal role in promoting female education, contributing to the progress of the people in Mysore province.

Wesleyan Mission- Pioneer of Education of Marginalized communities

Just as women were deprived of education, depressed class people were also denied the same from time unknown. The introduction of Western education started breaking this obstacle, beginning from 19th century. The Christian Missions played a remarkable role in this change. The Wesleyan Mission played its part in promoting the education of Depressed and backward classes through its educational endeavors, right from the beginning, in Mysore province. For example, out of the four schools which the Mission started in Mysore city in 1840 three were exclusively meant for the depressed class children. This is the same story in many other Wesleyan Mission centres in Mysore province, also.

Apart from the work of Proclamation of the Gospel and educational work Wesleyan missionaries later embarked also on medical service, literature work and many other initiatives. A more detailed explanation about them is not within the scope of this study, however in the subsequent chapters where the work of the Wesleyan missionaries in CN area is focused a greater detail about their varied and comprehensive work will be provided.

The era of Rev. Hodson, 'Father of Mysore Mission' comes to an end

Hodson retired in 1878 and returned to England after years of dedicated service in Mysore province. It was Hodson who initiated/ pioneered the Mission work among the Kannada people and opened important Mission stations in many parts of Mysore province. Thompson noted: 'Thomas Hodson, with the exception of an interval of ten years in England, completed fifty years of service in India and was for twenty-five years Chairman of the Mysore District' (Thompson, p.140). It was he who revived the Wesleyan

Mission work and laid a strong foundation for its expansion in Mysore province. He was rightly recognized as the 'Father of Mysore Mission.' Hodson passed away in England in 1882.

Josiah Hudson succeeded Hodson as the Chairman of Mysore District. The work of the Wesleyan Mission progressed further.

CHAPTER – 3

Wesleyan Missionaries Enter Chamarajanagara

The Wesleyan missionaries who were based in Mysore city soon started visiting the neighboring villages and towns in the region from 1838. Thus Srirangapatna, French Rocks (now Pandavapura in Mandya district), Nanjanagud, Hunsur and Pandavapura became some of their regular destinations of evangelistic travels. Eventually tiny congregations sprung up in some of those places.

The missionaries appeared to have travelled up to Nanjanagud, the famed temple town on the east of Mysore in 1870. In 1874 on the same route missionaries traveled still further, visiting Kollegal, Malavalli and so on. However due to the remoteness of the place they were not able make it to Chamarajanagara, earlier than 1879. As per missionary records Wesleyan missionaries first entered Chamarajanagara in the 1879.

Wesleyan missionaries' first visit to Chamarajanagara, 1879

Mysore city was the centre of Wesleyan missionary work in southern Mysore province and it was from there a team of missionaries and catechists first visited and camped in CN town in April, 1879

(MDR, 1879, p.34). The team consisted of missionaries C.H. Hocken, H. Gulliford, native assistant missionary T. Luke and catechist Ebenezer Nathaniel. It was a 200-mile-long evangelistic tour which had covered main places like CN, Gundlupet, Yellandur, Shimsha and Malavalli.

Wesleyan Mission report of 1879 gives a detailed account on the first visit to CN. The high lights of that report include:

CN was a small town with a population of about 5000. The name Chamarajanagara was bestowed by Raja on learning that his father late Khasa Chamaraja Wodeyar was born there. Therefore, the Raja dedicated the town to his father's name to perpetuate his name. Thus, what was once called Arikotara became Chamarajanagara (CN).

Missionaries conducted a service in the main street and the catechist Ebenezer preached a powerful sermon. People listened to the sermon with rapt attention. One youth jumped on the missionaries angrily protesting but the rest of the people immediately silenced him. At the end of the service missionaries sold much Gospel literature. Missionaries felt greatly encouraged from their first ever visit to CN (MDR, 1879, pp. 35-36).

Mission station opened in CN town-1885 – Bhakti Siromani the first evangelist

Finding their first visit to CN very encouraging missionaries subsequently visited the area few more times. Finally, they decided to open a Mission station there. Two reasons prompted them to open a Mission station: firstly, they saw CN was a densely populated area and secondly, they wanted a Mission station which connected their work from north to south (MDR, 1886, p.28).

Thus in 1885 the Mission posted Bhakti Siromani as the evangelist based in CN town. It was reported that one Miss Harrison of Preptwich, Manchester of England started financially supporting the Mission work in CN. In 1886 a small congregation was formed in the town.

The story of Isaac Kangani – first Christian convert of CN area

The very first convert to Christian faith from CN area was Isaac Kangani. Interestingly he was not a Wesleyan Mission convert nor was he baptized in CN proper, although he was very much a native of the place. The Wesleyan Mission report of 1893 pp.10-11 and Findley and Holdsworth p.294 as well as Bishop Sargant's book "From Mission to Churches" give details of the interesting story of Isaac Kangani which may be summarized briefly as follows: Sometime around 1873, much before the Wesleyan Mission entered CN area, a young couple from Panchama keri ('untouchables' street) in CN town went to Ceylon to work in the estates. While working there they met the CMS Tamil Coolie Mission which was working among the estate coolies. Eventually the couple was attracted to Christian faith and took baptism.

The hard-working couple fast came up in life. Isaac Kangani became a supervisor in the estate. He gave good education to his children. However, as the years passed the couple increasingly started yearning to go back to their native place namely CN to be with their people. They were also very keen to share their new-found faith to all their kith and kin. After about 20 years in Ceylon when Kangani heard that there was now an evangelist stationed in his home town he corresponded with the evangelist about his plan to return. The evangelist, most likely K. Shadrach, arranged for a rented house for Kangani family to reside. Kangani returned to CN in 1893 with his wife, eight children and grand children (MDR 1893, pp. 10-11).

People in the 'Panchama keri' received Kangani family with a mixed feeling-some with curiosity, few with jealousy and some with suspicion. People saw everything better with Kangani's family, but their only grouse was that they were all a 'casteless' people now. Kangani on his part soon built a house. In one part of his house he opened a school. There was also a place for Christian worship in the house. Kangani provided good education to his children and admitted them in Wesleyan Mission boarding school in Bangalore. After a few months he revisited Ceylon but soon returned to make CN his permanent home.

Kangani's house became a nucleus of Christian activities where worship, Bible studies and school classes were held. In the small congregation which met at Kangani's house there was yet another family which had migrated to Ceylon, got baptized there, like Kangani family, and returned back to CN town.

Kangani's school was for both children as well as for adults. His married daughter, son-in-law and grandson were all among the first pupils of the school sitting in the same class together! Scripture class was one main part in the school routine.

Kangani and his wife lived as trail blazers of the Gospel till their death. They carried an amazing zeal to spread the Gospel and to plant the churches among their people. However the light that Kangani and his wife kindled in CN town did not grow or spread as a movement. For many years the little flock had a static number of only 10 full members, at time even less. This fact used to greatly depress the missionaries. Referring to the poor growth the missionaries sincerely wished that Christians were more aggressive in reaching people with Gospel since after all they live among their own people (MDR 1898, p. vii).

Hostilities and opposition to Mission work in early period

The first evangelist, Bhakti Siromani, stationed in CN town in 1885, had to face a great deal of hostilities. The evangelist had great difficulty in getting a rented place to reside. He also faced problems to secure drinking water (MDR 1886, p.28). There were constant hostilities against open air preaching. There was also recurring plague and cholera menace which was extremely devastating. The health of the evangelist totally collapsed within a few weeks and he had to return to Mysore city for recovery. He could return to CN only after a few months, in next year.

The evangelist usually used to visit surrounding villages on Gospel work during the forenoons and in the evenings he would concentrate his work more in the town. He used to make use of the magic lantern to illustrate Gospel stories which would attract people greatly. Evangelist's preaching was generally listened to attentively and there were also quite a number of enquirers. K. Shadrak, who was based in CN town as Evangelist during 1893 to 1896, was specially being acknowledged for his remarkable in depth knowledge of Hinduism.

In the year 1888 the first evangelist Bhakti Siromani was replaced by John Israel who served in CN for four years. His work followed the same pattern set by the first evangelist which included mainly preaching in the villages and town and distribution/sale of Gospel literature. Many became enquirers but hardly any one came forward for baptism. This situation continued for many years.

Wesleyan Mission embarks on pioneering educational work in CN area

After the initial period of work which comprised of mainly open-air preaching and sale/distribution of Gospel literature, the Wesleyan Mission embarked on educational work in CN villages. In 1888 i.e., exactly three years after the Mission station in CN opened, missionaries started two schools. This heralded a period of pioneering work of Wesleyan Mission in promoting literacy and education in CN area, a region which was otherwise very backward and steeped deep in illiteracy.

The first two Mission schools in CN area

The first mission school in CN area was established in Ramasamudram in 1888. It was a village adjacent to CN town. It goes to the credit of Wesleyan Mission pioneers for being their first school and for a long time it was credited to be the only female school in entire CN taluk.

It was the repeated appeal of the villagers which persuaded the missionaries to open the school in Ramasamudram. The missionaries noticed that the parents carried a great interest for their children's education. This encouraged the missionaries to further expand educational work.

The villagers of Ramasamudram financially supported the school. The classes were held at the village Chavadi close to the village temple premise. Villagers provided a rent free house to the Mission and promised to build a separate school building at the earliest. It is striking that in the first year, namely in 1888 there were as many as 40 female pupils, belonging to Brahmin, Lingayat, backward class and Muslim communities. The school also soon started getting annual grants from the State from 1891.

Mission starts the first English school in CN town-1888

In August 1888 the Mission started an English school in CN town. As in the case of the girl's school in Ramasamudram this school was also started after repeated appeal from the local people. The newly started English school in CN town became a good link to the missionaries to relate themselves with the local people. On their part the local people fully supported the expenses of running the school (MDR.1888.p xix).

In 1889 this single teacher English school in CN town had 18 pupils-7 in middle class, 5 in upper primary and 6 in lower primary. Out of 18 students 15 were Brahmin, two were other Hindu and one Muslim.

The first two Wesleyan Mission converts in CN - 1889

In 1889 two baptisms took place which may be perhaps noted as first two conversions in CN proper out of the Wesleyan Mission labour. As narrated in the earlier section they were not the first converts of CN since Isaac Kangani along with his family already had embraced Christian faith much earlier, some time in 1870s, in far off Ceylon where they were migrant workers (Refer to previous section).

Among the first two Wesleyan Mission converts in 1889 noted above one was a woman who was mother-in-law of the resident evangelist John Israel (MDR, 1889, Appendix-I, p. vii). The second one to be baptized was a Soliga man. The Soliga was touched by the concern and care shown towards him by the evangelist when he was very sick, which led him to embrace Christian faith. The report says the Soliga did not live for long after his conversion.

Among the first two Wesleyan Mission converts in 1889 noted above one was a woman who was mother-in-law of the resident evangelist John Israel (MDR, 1889, Appendix-I, p. vii). The second one to be baptized was a Soliga man. The Soliga was touched by the concern and care shown towards him by the evangelist when he was very sick, which led him to embrace Christian faith. The report says the Soliga did not live for long after his conversion.

Many enquirers but hardly any baptism

As the years passed people became more and more used to missionaries and to their preaching. Instances of violent dissent against missionary preaching were also considerably reducing, with the passing of time.

On their part the missionaries felt that the people had a strange mixture of friendliness and fear towards the missionaries (MDR, 1894, p. xvii). Generally, people heard to Gospel preaching with rapt attention, but they kept a distance avoiding too close a contact. Further the missionaries felt that although 'many heard the Gospel; their hearts were not yet moved to embrace it' (MDR 1896 p. xiii).

According to the reports even in 1890s the resident evangelist in CN town had no access to village well and access to barber shop and so on. Missionaries saw that the caste factor, namely the fear of getting 'polluted' continued to be strongly embedded in the minds of the people. This held them back to make a final decision to embrace Christian faith. Although the number of enquirers increased over the years, the baptisms were seldom or far in between. The Missionary reports of 1897 says that many were interested to join Christian faith but the fear of losing livelihood held them back (MDR, 1897, pp.9-10). In 1898 the missionaries explained the mind set of people as follows: "This Hinduism is like great weight around our necks; it crushes us" the disillusioned may say so but they do not come out (MDR, 1898, p. xiii). Many people especially youth want to join Christianity, but alas family ties do not allow (MDR,1919, p.66). This was the scenario of Mission work in CN area in late 1890s, after about 15 years of work there, with little result.

Congregation in CN town in1890–tiny but devout

The missionary report of 1890 gives the following statistics for the congregation in CN town:

Preaching place	1
Evangelist	1
Day school teachers	2
Full Members	6
Average worshippers	9
Number of schools	1
Total pupils in School	38

The little Christian flock in CN town used to assemble for worship in a small chapel in the town till 1893. However, after Isaac Kangani's return from Ceylon his newly built house in Panchama Keri became the place of worship for the local congregation, since it was more practical.

The congregation in CN town remained very tiny for years. In 1895 there were 10 full members and four on trial. In fact, many of the members were relatives of Kangani. Kangani and his wife were very zealous of their Christian faith and were very keen that their kith and kin will also join the Christian fold. However, that never happened. The congregation never grew larger for reasons not known. Kangani's wife passed away in 1897. It was reported that her death was greatly grieved not only by Christians but also by others in the village.

Although the missionaries were sad that the church in CN town did not grow much nevertheless, they always carried praise for the tiny flock. The missionaries were happy that the little flock was regular in worship, consistent in living and it was a true work of Grace. Isaac Kangani and his family were being given full credit to this (MDR, 1896, p.vii). Haigh reported of this congregation stating 'the seven members in this station have given us no cause of anxiety…. They live in love and worship regularly together' (MDR, 1892, p.11). Missionary Gulliford also had full of praise for the congregation. It was reported that the congregation was also equally good in Christian giving, be it class money, weekly offerings, thanks offerings, offerings to missionary fund etc (ref, MDR, 1896, p.vii).

In 1892 Haigh had this to say about the CN town congregation: 'our people live well, they give well, and they die well' (MDR, 1892 p.9).

Dwindling number of Christians

As the years passed, it was strange that the number of full members of the congregation steadily decreased, so much so in 1905 and 1906 there was no evangelist posted to CN town. While the situation here was continuing to be bleak and depressing, in a village not too far from CN town namely Kastur village a remarkable 'Christ ward movement' was about to be unfolding! This will be seen in detail in the next chapter.

Recurring plague, cholera and famine

Recurring plague, cholera and famine had been a regular feature in CN area, perhaps from time unknown. While deforestation and the consequent failure of rainfall created a chronic famine condition, the fatal diseases like plague, cholera and influenza constantly inflicted people due to scarcity of water/ drinking water, primitive sanitation, lack of health awareness, malnutrition etc. The toll which those diseases used to take each time was often very high. The tiny Christian flock of CN town also suffered from famine, natural calamities and fatal diseases very much. Under these circumstances, obviously, the mission work too suffered constant setbacks.

The Evangelists who served in CN town congregation – 1885 to 1908

The Mission station which was opened in CN town in 1885 was part of Mysore Circuit for long. For initial many years all the expenses were met by Miss. Harrison of Manchester, England. From 1909 the expenses were met by the District Mission Fund which was a fund raised by local contributions from English and native members.

Following is the list of pioneer evangelists who served CN town congregation from the year station started there in 1885 until 1910:

Name of the Evangelists and the years they served in CN town congregation (now named as Tomlinson Memorial church)

(1885-1910)

Bhakti siromani	1885-1886
John Israel	1888-1891
H. Anandappa	1892
K. Shadrak	1893-1896
A. Masilamani	1897-1898

A. Sanjeeva (Reader)	1899
Chintamani Caleb	1900
Clement Caleb	1901-1904
Vacant	1905-1906
R. Bhaktivrutha	1907-1908
D. Sathyanatha	1909-1910

(Source: Mysore District Reports (MDR)

CHAPTER – 4

A Chronicle of Church Planting in Chamarajanagara Villages

Period: 1908 – 1947

The year 1908 is an important milestone in the history of Christianity in CN area. It heralded the beginning of a remarkable 'Christ ward movement' which spread into many villages with Kastur village as the epicenter. Also named as 'Kastur Movement' it continued for three to four decades, almost until mid 1940s.

Kastur is located about 10 kilometers north of CN town. The baptism of eight adults and five children which took place in this village on 14th September 1908 triggered a chain of response with eventually a large number of families embracing Christian faith in Kastur and other villages. After years of 'drought' of conversion, for more than two decades, the missionaries' joy knew no bound when an unexpected 'harvest' began forthcoming, beginning from Kastur village!

Rev. George William Sawday (1854-1944) – The pioneer church planter of CN area

It was unquestionably Rev. George William Sawday who was the pioneer and the master planter of churches in CN villages! Christians in this region even today remember this legendary missionary with utmost respect and with great nostalgia. Most of the churches in CN area as well as dozens of churches in Mysore, Mandya, Tumkur, and Bangalore and in many other places are named after this great missionary Sawday. He served as a Wesleyan missionary in India almost his whole life time, first in Tumkur area and later most of his life time in Mysore region.

The outstanding work of Sawday in Mysore province, especially his pivotal role in the planting of churches in CN area will be seen in detail in a separate chapter later. It all began in Kastur, in 1908.

The Story of Mudda and Mada

In Wesleyan Mission report of 1908 Sawday vividly describes in detail what really had transpired in the little village of Kastur. Following is a brief summary:

Two young brothers Mudda and Mada of Kastur village had in early 1900s migrated to Wayanad to work in coffee estates. Sawday stated that the brothers were 'two young men belonging to a very respectable family of Panchamas' in Kastur (MDR, 1908, p.v). The family was also well of, economically.

While working in the estate the brothers met the Basel missionaries who were working there. They were also attending a night school run by Basel Mission. Eventually both the brothers who were attracted towards Christian faith made up their mind to take baptism. At first the elder brother took the baptism (MDR.1908, p. 50, also 1933, p. 4). When this news reached their home in Kastur the agitated parents implored their sons to return home, immediately. The brothers had to concede to their parents' demand and reluctantly returned to Kastur.

Back in their village they took up to their old faith again since there was no opportunity in their village to practice their new-found Christian religion. However, both the brothers were feeling deeply disturbed within, all the time. They were both well educated for their class. Together they studied many sacred books and visited various pilgrim centres in search of truth, salvation and peace of mind. But they were disillusioned. They did not find either salvation or any hope in them. They continued their search for the true faith, unceasingly.

It was during this time Mada came to know about the evangelist Shadrack of Wesleyan Mission, based in CN town. He started to visit the evangelist regularly to spend long hours with him to share his spiritual struggles. Finally, after a long search and struggle both the brothers made a final decision to re-embrace Christian faith.

It was reported that two reasons hastened them to make the final decision for conversion. Firstly, their final total disillusion with Hinduism and secondly, a bitter caste humiliation which Mada experienced at the hands of a Brahmin at the evangelist Shadrach's house in CN town. According to the report when once Mada entered the evangelist's house the evangelist was conversing with a Brahmin visitor. When the evangelist asked Mada to sit, apparently by the side of Brahmin, the latter in great disgust and with cursing words went out fearing ritual pollution from Mada (MDR, 1933, p.4)! It was an unbearable humiliation.

Evangelist J.L. Jonathan- "The Pioneer Missionary of Mysore Church"

The news about the two 'seeker' brothers and their spiritual struggles were reaching Sawday based in Mysore. Foreseeing the possibility of a good break through Sawday immediately posted an evangelist, J.L. Jonathan to Kastur village.

Jonathan was financially supported by the native fund namely, District Extension Fund till 1911. Afterwards Mysore Missionary Society which was formed as per the decision of Wesleyan Synod became the supporting body of Kastur work (Bodhaka Bodhini, February 1911, p.38).

Jonathan, who hailed from Hassan, had been acclaimed as the 'Pioneer Missionary of Mysore church' because of his many years of tireless and pioneering labour in Kastur and surrounding villages. He was the first native missionary supported entirely by native funds! It was Jonathan who under the guidance of Sawday did a remarkable service as a facilitator of the Christ ward movement which was beginning in Kastur and slowly spreading to other villages. Jonathan's service was greatly acknowledged and appreciated by Sawday, often. Being very happy about a growing tiny congregation full of life, Sawday exclaimed: 'This has been owing largely to the devoted labours of Jonathanayya and his fellow evangelists' (MDR, 1910, p.32). After serving many years in CN villages and Mysore circuit Jonathan retired. He passed away in 1942.

First baptisms in Kastur

Sawday, observing the possibility of a good 'harvest' immediately posted a Bible Woman to assist the evangelist in Kastur. The evangelist and the Bible Woman together as a team did a remarkable work in preparing the candidates for baptism, meticulously. On 14-9-1908 eight adults and five children were received into Christian faith through baptism given by Sawday. Baptized candidates included:

Muddaiah and Madaiah's parents: Channappa (Chriatian name **Gurudasa**) and Basamma (renamed, **Lydiamma)**

Muddaiah's wife Muddamma (renamed, **Bhagyamma**),

Madaiah (renamed **Devadas**) and his wife Madamma (renamed, **Sanjeevamma**),

Madaiah's servant Mayappa (renamed, **Peter,** 17 years),

Muddappa (renamed, **Gurubhakta**) and wife Boramma (renamed, **Sathyamma**).

Number of totally baptized-8 adults.

(Source: Register of Adult Baptisms, Wesleyan Mission, Chamarajanagara)

Muddaiah was not among those baptized on 14-9-1908 since he had already taken the baptism in Wayanad when he was working in estates. Among the children who were baptized included, Muddaiah and Madaiah families two children each and Gurubhakta and Satyamma's one child. Thus 8 adults and 5 children were baptized on 14th September 1908 in Kastur.

After the baptism Muddaiah became **Abraham** and Madaiah became **Devadas.**

Commotion in Kastur protesting baptisms

Sawday reports that there was a huge crowd to watch the baptisms taking place; this was because the brothers had sent word to all their relations in all the villages around Kastur (MDR, 1908, p.52). The brothers wanted their decision, to become Christians, to be known widely to everyone. It was a tension-filled event which stirred up Kastur and surrounding villages. There was much commotion created by caste Hindus against conversions, but the protest was dealt very firmly by Sawday, Devadas and others.

Baptisms in Bhogapura

On 15th September 1908 i.e., the very next day the baptisms took place in Kastur, three persons in Bhogapura joined Christian fold through the baptism given by Sawday. Bhogapura was a village adjacent to Kastur. The three baptized on 15th September included a woman, Mariamma (earlier, Basamma) and her two children (Source: **Register of Adult Baptisms**). Her husband Isaac was baptized earlier while he was working in estates in Wayanad.

The Baptisms in both Kastur and Bhogapura villages created a great deal of commotion in the villages. The agitated caste Hindus tried hard to create disturbance to prevent the baptisms taking place. However, Sawday and Devadas (old name Madaiah) stood firm and dealt with the protestors firmly and saw that the baptism event concluded peacefully.

The Mission reports state that on18th October i.e. within about a month after the first three baptisms, Bhogapura witnessed few more baptisms, with five adults and seven children joining the Christian fold.

Abraham (Mudda) and Devadas (Mada)- leaders of young congregations

Abraham, the first convert of Kastur was working as a tailor, besides agriculture. He was a good reader of books for his class. Villagers used to call him as 'Upadru' (means teacher or guru) because of his good deal of knowledge on religions and on other matters.

Devadas was endowed with remarkable leadership qualities. Eventually he became a good leader of the new Christian community in the area and an entrepreneur. He was also known to be a generous donor and a philanthropist. Devadas worked, shoulder to shoulder, with the missionaries, especially Sawday, and thus played an important role in the planting/expansion of the village churches in the CN area (refer Chapter VII for more details on Abraham and Devadas).

Gospel reaches Mangalada Hosur, Homma and few other villages

The Christ ward movement which started in **Kastur** and then in **Bhogapura** in 1908 very soon spread to several other surrounding villages. First to reach was the large village **Mangalada Hosur** (here after M. Hosur). This village had one of the largest markets in the area in those days. In 1910 there were baptisms in **Homma**. In March 1910 eight adults and twelve children, and in May same year seven adults and four children and in December one adult were baptized in Homma forming a congregation there.

By 1910 there were a total of 55 adults and 42 children baptized in four CN villages namely Kastur, Bhogapura, M. Hosur and Homma. The Gospel was fast spreading into furthermore villages.

In 1910 there were few baptisms in **Doddarayanapet** and **Kiragsur** villages.

Work demanding infinite patience and love

By 1910 few tiny congregations in and around Kastur were formed. Findley and Holdsworth had made a touching observation: 'For some years nothing more transpired, but in 1908 Mr. Sawday was able to baptize thirty-eight persons from these villages, and every year since has witnessed the growth of the little church thus formed. Much work, a demanding infinite patience, and the love which creates confidence and trust, was necessary before these timid villagers, who had been brought under the domination of persons belonging to a higher caste, could be emboldened to give themselves to Christ' (Findley and Holdsworth, p.294).

Sawday begins the mission of 'redeeming' children from slavery

As the Kastur movement began to spread into many villages one of the shocking discoveries Sawday had was the rampant prevalence of Jitha or slavery. He saw that a little borrowing of money from village money lender in their emergency often led people into debt trap and ultimately pushing them into lifelong slavery. Most of those who were pushed into slavery were the people of depressed classes.

What disturbed Sawday most was how even small boys and girls of tender age were pushed into slavery. For Sawday who had by nature a very affectionate heart towards children could not bear the sight of children suffering lifelong inhuman slavery. It became dilemma for Sawday to see parents converted but children still in slavery (MDR, 1911, p.41). This led him to embark on a mission of redeeming slave children along with the church planting work. The redemption of slave children was not an easy task but a stupendous one since it included tough negotiations with the money lenders/land lords, requiring huge amount to redeem children and the mortgaged lands and look after the children's future including providing education to them and so on. Sawday accomplished this mission unceasingly during his time of active ministry and redeemed scores of children from slavery. This was the path breaking work which immensely helped in the growth and witness of the church in CN villages

District Evangelistic Band under Tomlinson–a great boon to Mission work

In 1910 a District Evangelist Band was appointed by the Wesleyan Mission. This became a great boon especially to the fast picking up of work in the CN villages. The first District Evangelist was none other than Rev. W. E. Tomlinson (1897-1944), a pioneer Wesleyan missionary of great repute, who was working shoulder to shoulder with Sawday in Mysore and CN circuits. In fact, the very formation of the Band itself was Tomlinson's initiative. Tomlinson was heading the Band and had four native evangelists with him to help in the evangelistic itinerary, in the entire region, including Mysore, CN, and Mandya and so on. It was a tiring and exacting work, constantly on the move. Tomlinson's team of touring evangelists, gave an excellent support to the catechists and evangelists working in the villages and thus became a great blessing to the Kastur movement.

The unexpected and quite rapid church growth compelled the Wesleyan Mission to appoint a greater number of evangelists, catechists and Bible Women in CN area to cope up with the pressing need.

Growing opposition, drought and diseases

The caste Hindu opposition against the missionary work which was erupted during baptisms in Kastur and Bhogapura, was dormant for some time, but it never fully subsided at any time, at all. As the Mission work actively carried on in many villages, the opposition too became increasingly vociferous, even violent. The Hindu orthodox elements in Mysore, Nanjanagud and elsewhere began to instigate caste Hindus in CN area against the missionaries. A section of vernacular press added fuel to the agitation through its malicious propaganda, poisoning the minds of gullible people. Under this circumstance the missionaries, neo converts and even enquirers had to face untold difficulties at every step. Harassment and even persecution of neo converts and missionaries became order of the day.

In 1911 the missionaries reported: 'Early in the year some enquirers were severely beaten by their masters, and this act of intimidation had its effect on the people, who are naturally timid and easily frightened' (MDR, 1911, p.41). In fact, the growing violent opposition led missionaries to give a temporary break to expansion work but to concentrate more on consolidation (Ibid).

If violent harassment was one thing the neo converts had to constantly and increasingly face, there was also the problem of chronic drought and diseases which were devastating (refer Chapter on Persecution, Drought and Diseases). In 1912 missionaries wrote: 'Death had been busy, sickness was still rife, and the crops had failed' (MDR, 1912, p.34). Paying tribute to people's unshakable faith the missionaries added' they silently suffered, but not murmured'.

Breakthrough in Madigahalli (Madapura)

Two families with six adults were baptized in **Madigahalli** (later named as Madapura) in 1914. Gnana giriappa and Gurusisiddhappa were heads of those two families who were the first converts in that village. Due to fear of Lingayat backlash there were no further baptisms in Madapura for next few years. In 1921 four leading families of Madapura got converted and with this the congregation began to grow faster (Harvest Field, 1921, pp.316-318). The W.M. Register of Baptisms has documented that there were again 32 adult baptisms and of some children in 1921, in this village.

In 1915 six adults and few children were baptized in **Singonapura**. In 1916 two adults in **Honnali** village and two in **Kallalli** were baptized.

Missionary nostalgia of Kastur church

Kastur village and church always carried a great deal of nostalgic feelings in missionaries. It was the Kastur baptisms in 1908 that ended a long 'drought' of souls and ignited a rapid spread of the Good News in CN villages. Eight years after first baptisms in Kastur, in 1916 Sawday happily reported:

'Eight years not long in the life of a people, but there can be few places in the world where greater changes have taken place in the hearts and lives of the people eight years after first conversions in Kastur...' (MDR, 1916, p.31).

A new church building in Kastur

Ever since the Kastur congregation was formed in 1908, worship used to be conducted in a thatched hall. In 1916 that place of worship was replaced with a church building. That was the first church built in entire CN area. People's joy knew no bound on the occasion of dedication of the new church. Besides Sawday, there were also missionary Rees, native ministers Luke and Samuel Lamech. Many from neighboring village congregations and a contingent of Christians from Mysore city were also part of the joyous event.

The Kastur church building was renovated/ extended in 1991 and again in 2008 renovated at the time of centenary.

A congregation in Masgapura

Next it was the turn of **Masgapura**, a village few kilometers north of CN town. In 1917 twelve adults and few children were baptized in Masgapura. There were more baptisms in this village in 1945 with 25 newly baptized.

Not a mass movement but a movement... it moves

Missionaries were happy that since the Kastur baptisms in 1908 the Good News was spreading in the area and small congregations were forming. However, the missionaries' expectation of a mass conversion of people like that happened in Andhra or Tamil country was not taking place in CN area/Mysore province. In fact, this was a much-debated subject in the Mission circle. Often missionaries concluded Mysore province had fewer conversions because of the conservative mind set of people and they were very much controlled by Hindu orthodoxy, far more than in other states. In Centenary report in 1921 the missionaries noted: 'for Kanarese temperament is very conservative and unimpressionable (contrasting, for instance, with that of the alert, progressive Tamil),...' (MDR,1921,p.45). They also added that the fairly prosperous conditions in agricultural life for about nine-tenth of the population tend to make them religiously conservative. In the meanwhile, the missionaries had to content with the work in CN area/ Mysore province which they thought 'not a mass movement but a movement, it moves.' (MDR, 1939, p.4).

More village churches planted – more caste Hindu opposition

Hardya (later renamed as Hadya) is a large village located about 20 kilometers west of Kastur. With the baptism of eleven adults and few children in 1922 the foundation of a congregation was laid. There were more conversions in 1939 but a very violent opposition followed, with determined efforts to win the newly converted back to old religion.

The orthodox Hindus were increasingly disturbed to see outcaste defections from Hinduism under the very shadow of sacred hill (i.e. Chamundi Hill). Therefore, they set all of kinds obstacles before those people (MDR, 1923, p.9).

In 1923 fourteen adults were baptized in **Kirugunda.** This was a village closer to Hadya on the one side and the temple town Nanjanagud on the other. Like in Hadya conversions in Kirugunda also immediately ignited violent protest the neo converts and the missionaries. Ironically, those who were protesting, and instigating violence were 'Gandhians' or freedom fighters. It was none but one 'highly held' freedom fighter' Thagadur Ramachandra Shastri who was leading a penchant crusade everywhere in Mysore-CN areas against Christian missionaries! Agitators offered tempting monetary promises in dissuading the enquirers and the newly baptized to relapse. Mission reports say that despite all the odds Sawday, Devadas and missionary Stanley Edward, son –in-law of Sawday boldly faced the situation and stood by with the vulnerable neo converts. Reporting on the great commotion prevailed on baptism day in Kirugunda the missionaries reported: 'It was a high day for the Christians, who had gathered from all directions' (MDR,1923, p.53).

Kunnaiah (Christian name, Gurushanthappa), the chieftain of Holeya) community in **Kerehalli** was baptized in 1923. Few more baptisms took place shortly after that laying the foundation of a congregation in that village. Gurushanthappa was threatened and assaulted by caste Hindus but he stood remarkably firm till the end (ref. Chapter VII, for furthermore about Gurushanthappa).

Establishment of hospital, Ashram and schools in Kastur/ CN area

In 1922 Sawday opened a hospital in Kastur. Started as a small hospital very soon it made a great name attracting patients from far and wide. Due to the dedicated service it offered it became a remarkable healing centre for the entire region. In 1925 Sawday opened an Ashram for women in Kastur as a women resource centre for the entire region. The Ashram was called as 'Premalaya'.

It was from this centre that a remarkable work was done among women and children of the region. On the other hand, the mission opened many schools, even in remote villages. Schools were open to all people, irrespective of caste and creed.

The contribution made by the hospital and Ashram was inestimable, greatly supporting the Mission work and the growth of the church in CN villages.

National freedom movement- Missionaries / Christian community under attack

India was increasingly becoming restive after 1880s with independent spirit growing. Missionaries noticed that even among Christians, independence spirit was growing. The Freedom Movement was spreading like wild fire after 1920 especially after Swadeshi movement started under the leadership of Gandhiji.

It was ironical that along with the growth of independence/ national spirit a strong anti-Christian feeling was also developing in Mysore province. Christian Mission work was equated to British imperialism. Their anti-British Raj animosity was expressed in anti-Christian and anti- Western feelings (MDR, 1924, p.5). The missionaries and the entire Mission work were seen as anti- Indian and became an object of much dislike and contempt (Sargant, pp.14-15).

Missionaries generally carried a good regard towards Gandhi. His deep admiration for Christ, Christian tenets especially Bible was very much appreciated by the missionaries. However as far as national freedom movement was concerned missionaries nursed some reservations. They often argued that nationalism was good but not overdoing of it. They thought that hatred of other religions and missionaries were not good. It was ironical that with the spread of national freedom movement, communalism/ religious violence and strong anti-Christian Mission feeling was escalating, leaps and bounds. Obviously, all those developments had very detrimental effect on Mission work, even in CN area.

Gospel reaches Kellamballi and few other villages

In 1924 in **Kellamballi** village, 9 kilometers west of CN town, eleven adults and a child took baptism. Also, in 1924 there was baptism of an adult in **Annalli** and baptism of three adults and a child in **Kallalli.**

In 1927 an adult took baptism in **Bisselwadi**. Eventually, with few more joining a tiny congregation came into being.

Basavatti, a large village in the north witnessed baptism of sixteen adults and nine children in June 1929. In December same year there were baptism of three adults and three children.

Baptisms in Mandya and Kadalur - A big boost to Mission work

On 30th November 1924 **Mandya**, an upcoming town north of Mysore city on Mysore-Bangalore highway, witnessed a large number of 64 people being baptized (Sargant, pp.16 and 19 and HF, 1925, p.35).This rich 'harvest' was outcome of years of labour of Wesleyan Mission evangelists and missionaries. The enquirers had to suffer much harassment for a long period including verbal abuse and stone throwing on their place of residence and worship. Vernacular media based in Mysore made an extensive false propaganda on Mission work in Mandya (MDR, 1924, pp.58-59).

However, withstanding all opposition, on November 1924 Sawday baptized 64 people in Mandya. A huge commotion erupted in the town on the day. However, Sawday together with the evangelists bravely faced the situation. An evangelist to be remembered in the whole episode was one Jeremiah David, who with great courage and commitment faced all the onslaughts and meticulously prepared the enquirers for Baptism. David, who hailed from Coorg from Basel Mission background, was serving the Wesleyan Mission as an evangelist in Mysore, Mandya and CN region.

The very next year of Mandya baptisms, i.e. on November 15th, 1925 Sawday baptized 66 persons in **Kadalur,** a large village further north of Mandya. Kadalur people were related to the neo converts in Mandya through marriages. That was the reason why people in Kadalur became enquirers. Although Mandya and Kadalur were not part of CN area the remarkable breakthrough in those two places of neighboring region gave an immense boost to the briskly ongoing Mission work in CN area.

Gospel reaches more villages

In 1931 there was an adult baptism in **Ummathu**r a village close to CN town. In olden times this village used to be the capital of Palegar rulers of CN area.

A large harvest was reaped in **Ugani** (also known as Kodi Ugani), a village closer to southern border. Twenty-three adults and twenty-four children were baptized in May 1931.

Next it was **Heggevadi**'s turn, on the west of the CN town, closer to Kerehalli and Mudnakod villages. People of Heggewadi village were all belonged to depressed class. In 1931 thirty-eight people (19 adults and 19 children) were baptized in Heggevadi.

Kamarvadi, a village near Basavatti had three adults baptized in 1931.

Sawday retires from active service

Sawday retired from service in 1931. He was born in England in 1854, came as a missionary to India/ Mysore province in 1876. His first station was Kunigal and after that he worked in Tumkur beginning from 1877, during the Great Famine period. After an astounding tenure of service in Tumkur for several years, faced with a series tragic death of his two infant daughters he returned to England in 1894. However, there was no respite for tragic events in his life. His wife passed away the same year in England. Eventually, Sawday began working as a Methodist pastor. However, his beloved India was beckoning him, and he returned to this country in 1900, having been posted to Mysore city.

Sawday's long tenure of over three decades (1900-1931) in Mysore region turned out to be a golden age of Wesleyan Mission work in Mysore province, especially of Mysore and CN circuits!

Even after his retirement from active service Sawday continued to be involved in the growth of the churches actively as a mentor, counselor and builder, till the very end (ref. Chapter X on Sawday for more details).

Tomlinson, Sargant, Hill and many dedicated Indian ministers took the mantle and continued with the work to which the Wesleyan Mission was dedicated to.

More villages reached with the Gospel

In 1933 an adult joined the Christian fold in **Dodda Homma (Homma).**

In 1934 a group of 11 people were baptized in **Andrakalli,** a village close to Madigahalli (Madapura). The group included eight adults and three children.

Bedarapura a large village west of CN town reaped a good harvest of twelve adults joining the Christian fold in 1935.

The year 1936 witnessed four adults baptized in **Kuderu**, eight adults in **Deshavalli** and nine in **Kalkunda.** The village **Mudnakod** a village in south west of CN town, witnessed few baptisms in 1936. A larger group of 51 persons joined the Christian fold in this village, later in1946.

Ankusharayanapura was a village between Kastur and Homma. In 1938 ten adults took baptism and thus a small congregation came into being.

Fire accident in Kellamballi in 1938

In 1938 there was a serious fire accident in Kellamballi in which many huts /houses including six which belonged to Christian families were totally burnt down. Agriculture implements and stored grain were also burnt down pushing families into destitution. As this news reached Mysore city Christians, they decided to lend a helping hand to their brethren in the village. Essential aid was immediately rushed to Kellamballi in kind and cash, all of which very timely helped the fire victim families to rehabilitate themselves. Further it was heartening that several village congregations in the area also joined hands in the relief work contributing their 'mite' (MDR, 1938, p.23).

It was indeed a sign of exemplary Christian witness that the relief aid was not only given to Christian families but to all the families in distress in that village, irrespective of caste and creed.

Phenomenal mission work in CN area – greatly acclaimed all over

In 1938 the CN circuit had 16 staff i.e., native ministers, evangelists, Bible Women and catechists. Such a large number was totally unforeseen! At one stage there were four Bible Women in the area stationed in different places of CN area. The evangelists used to regularly visit villages 2-3 times a week to sow the 'seeds of life'. The church members used to voluntarily join the evangelists in those visits to villages. The overflowing enthusiasm of the new believers was an inspiration and a great source of strength for the missionaries.

Besides, missionaries, evangelists and Bible Women there were number of lay leaders who played a pivotal part in the planting of churches in CN area. They were called as lay missionaries or 'unofficial evangelists' in Mission reports, in those days (refer the separate chapter vii in this volume on some of the lay missionaries and their remarkable service).

A well-organized pastoral work, preaching and teaching, educational and medical work gave a much-needed support to the growth of the churches in CN area (refer chapter VIII, on Empowerment).

The Missionary reports of the time noted with overwhelming joy that in no other circuit of the entire Mysore province (which included Bangalore, Mysore, Tumkur, Hassan, Chikamagalur, and Chitradurga etc.) surpassed the growth rate of CN circuit both in number of staff and number of conversions! The Wesleyan Mission work in CN villages acquired a great significance, all over, due to the remarkable success it achieved in the region during the period between 1910s to mid 1940s.

'Panchama Church' of CN area- minister of God's Grace

The missionaries were more than happy about the progress in work in CN area. The work in the area was catching wide attention, all over! Since almost all converts were from outcaste social origin the missionaries appreciatively addressed it as the

'Panchama Church'. They toiled in the area tirelessly with the partnership of a dedicated band of Indian workers and lay people. The evangelistic spirit of the newly converted was inexplicably amazing. That further inspired the missionaries to give their best for the cause of the Gospel.

Rejoicing about the 'Panchama Church' Sawday reported in 1921, "...it may be that a saved and regenerate outcaste church of Christ may be the minister of God's Grace to the India of the future." (MDR, 1921, p.46). Indeed, a great prophetic hope.

Silver Jubilee of Kastur church-1933

In 1933 the 'Mother Church' namely, the Kastur church celebrated its Silver Jubilee. It was a grand event with about 1000 people from most of the village congregations in the area participating in it. From each village came Christians. A huge pandal was built for the purpose. About 700 people marched in the village in a long procession holding banners and singing. Tomlinson was the main preacher. Sawday, who was already retired from active service was very much present on the memorable occasion and addressed the gathering (MDR, 1933, p.5). Sawday's lifelong friend evangelist Samuel Lamech was also active part of the celebration.

The church in Kastur village, from where the flame of Good News first ignited and spread into several villages, grew further. By the end of 1930s almost the entire depressed class community in Kastur had turned to Christ (MDR, 1938, p.7). In the first half of the 20th century more than a dozen pastors and evangelists hailed from Kastur only, and thus as the 'Mother Church' it made a remarkable contribution in the growth of the churches in CN area.

While the church in Kastur lived faithful to her Calling, growth of this infant church was not without pangs of pain. Pastoral care of this church as well as other infant village congregations was a stupendous task for the missionaries as well as the residential evangelists. The missionary reports of mid 1920s tell about long drawn factions in Kastur church, which was finally settled, and peace and harmony prevailed (MDR, 1925, p.55).

In 1938 the Kastur church celebrated its 30th anniversary. It was a memorable event. Sawday, the founder of this church, now retired from active service, was very much present at the grand occasion. Sixteen people took baptism in the special worship. With that only three families in Kastur remained in old faith but they were also in the list of enquirers (MDR, 1938, p.7)

Conversions in Hadya and the subsequent turmoil -1939

Early in 1939 a large number of 55 people were baptized in Hadya. Immediately there was a big uproar by caste Hindus, as usual, backed by the Hindu orthodoxy. The neo converts were severely threatened and harassed to return back to their old religion. They were also induced with material benefits. Prospective enquirers were threatened and intimidated. Amidst the big outcry the agitators managed to force 35 newly baptized persons to relapse into old religion. However, one family among the relapsed, to which belonged a community leader, returned back to Christian fold (MDR, 1939, p.4).

Death of Mysore Maharaja Nalvadi Krishnaraja Wodeyar-1940

Nalvadi Krishnaraja Wodeyar, the ruler of Mysore province passed away on August 3, 1940. He was enthroned in 1895 when he was 11 years old. His mother ruled as regent but from 1902 he took up the reins. A very progressive and benevolent ruler he was held in high respect by all the sections of the population. The countless constructive measures and projects which he had executed including judicial and administrative reforms, educational, industrial and irrigational works, dawned a new era of progress in Mysore province. He was a devout Hindu, but he respected all religions equally. He was very secular and democratic in his governance. Respected by many as a 'philosopher-king', the Mysore province was widely acclaimed as the 'best ruled Indian state' during his tenure.

Nalvadi Krishnaraja Wodeyar always carried a high appreciation for Christian missionary work especially their educational and medical endeavors. He patronized and liberally donated to many of their works. He had a great respect for Sawday and had a cordial relationship with him.

Wodeyar's death was deeply mourned not only in Mysore province but people from far and wide. It was a rare honor that it was Sawday who was invited to preside over the Public Condolence Meeting held in Bangalore.

Growing spirit of unity and resistance among Christians

It was striking that Christians were increasingly developing a strong sense of unity and spirit of resistance. In 1916 when a few enquirers were about to take baptism the leader of that group was kidnapped and kept in house arrest in a distant place. At that time a large detachment of new believers went to the place and barge into the hiding place and brought him back! It was reported as a daring act of unity and resistance (MDR, 1915, p.15).

During the Kirgunda turmoil in 1923 the resistance and unity shown by the new community was remarkable. It was striking that when the Christians in that village were under serious threat, Christians in neighboring villages did not remain silent spectators or docile but stood in solidarity with the people who were under threat. Missionaries very much appreciated the growing unity and the spirit of resistance which were developing in the young congregations. Referring to the Kirugunda turmoil the missionaries reported 'while we sorrow about relapse, we greatly joy over resistance shown by Christian families and rallying of Christians of surrounding villages' (MDR, 1939.p.4).

"Community movements" in CN villages – the recommendations of Synod Commission -1941

A ten-member Synod Commission visited CN circuit for inspection in 1941. The commission appreciated the phenomenal work carried on in CN villages and made some concrete recommendations for further progress. The Commission opined that the conversion movement which was continued taking place in CN villages was part of a 'community movement'. The Commission felt that the work should be further strengthened. It also recognized the remarkable work done by Sawday in redeeming scores of children from jitha/slavery. The Commission recommended that the Mission should start an active public campaign for the abolition of jitha/slavery and also a lobbying at the governmental level (MDR, 1941, pp.38ff).

Gospel reaches southern parts bordering Tamil country

It may be noted that almost all the churches planted from the year 1908 to 1930s were in the eastern part and few in western part of the CN area/taluk. However, from late 1930s the Mission started actively working in the villages of southern part of the area too. As a result, the Mission started reaping a good harvest in that part of the area.

Those new villages of south which were reached by the Mission did not exactly belonged to the erstwhile CN taluk/Mysore province but to Talwadi firka of Satyamangala taluk under Madras Presidency or 'Kumpani' territory. Most of the people in those border villages were Kannada speaking. The area was covered with thick forests and infested with wild animals. Besides, with very poor infrastructure, the accessibility to those villages was extremely difficult. This condition prevails to a great extent even now. Besides, due to rampant poverty and illiteracy the area was at the lowest level in all human development indexes.

From early 1940s missionaries in their outreach came closer to Mysore- Tamil country border in the south and soon crossed over to above noted 'kumpani' territory. In 1940 a congregation in **Mettluvad**i was formed with the baptism of ten adults and thirteen children. Roman Catholics and Faith/Brethren Mission were quite active in this place, earlier to Wesleyans; the Roman Catholics were quite active particurly in Gajanur, Tiganare and Mettluvadi from 1920s. However, during the WW-II the work of the Catholic Mission greatly weakened after its leading missionary Brother Romulus of enemy country was detained by the British. Faith Mission too was facing some organizational problems. It was at this time the Wesleyan Mission began to make some gains.

One Gurusiddhappa of Metluvadi who married a girl from Bhogapura was the first convert, in fact for the entire Talwadi region. He was a tailor and a cloth merchant. It was due to his initiative his relative Jayaprabhu of Tiganare joined the Christian fold laying the foundation of a congregation in remote **Tiganare** village in 1942. Jayaprabhu was a school teacher.

Same year the remote **Singanapura** witnessed baptism of four adults and three children. More conversions took place in Singanapura in 1947 with twenty-one adults and some children joining the Christian fold.

In **Tiganare** there was a much bigger harvest when in 1942 twenty-five adults took baptism. This village, part of a very backward region, had an alarming number of about 100 cases of leprosy in 1940s. The place was also infested with constant menace of elephants. As noted earlier, Gurusiddappa, the first Christian of Mettluvadi, was instrumental in planting the congregation in Tiganare. Among the newly converted there were few Roman Catholic families also, who were left behind without pastoral care in their church (MDR, 1942, 9).

In 1943 Faith Mission's **T. Hosur** and **Gajanu**r congregations were handed over to Wesleyan Mission and became part of it. The Mission report states: 'Mr. A. E. Perkins of the Brethren Mission who has graciously handed over work and sold us his little chapel at Gajanur' (MDR,1944, p12).

Those two congregations also saw two adults and in T. Hosur six adults joining Christian fold the same year. Faith Mission had some serious difficulties in managing its congregations in Talwadi region during that time. Under this circumstance as noted earlier the Mission voluntarily handed over few of its congregations to Wesleyan Mission.

In **Karalavadi,** a remote village in Talwadi region saw a larger harvest in same year i.e.1943. Including twenty-one adults and the rest children a total of 40 took baptism in 1943 in this village. Missionaries were preparing those people for baptism since 1942 (MDR, 1943, p. 10).

In 1943 the missionaries entered yet another village, **Kottanahall**i, located in yet an extremely inaccessible and difficult area, infested with contagious diseases and wild animals. There was a thirty-five-member congregation in Kottanahalli in 1943. It was reported however that there was a serious malaria outbreak same year due to which ten members died and nine members relapsed to Hindu religion (Sargant, p.60 and MDR, 1943, p. 10).

In some of the congregations of this border area few Catholic families too had joined the Wesleyan congregations since the Catholic missionaries were also undergoing crisis in maintaining and provide proper pastoral care to the congregations, in this region, at that World War II period.

Death of Tomlinson and Sawday-1944–End of a great era

The year 1944 turned out to be the year of great loss through deaths of several veterans. Tomlinson, who worked shoulder to shoulder with Sawday passed away on 29th August 1944. His death was very untimely. He collapsed while playing tennis. He was 67 years old when he died. It was Tomlinson who played a pivotal role in providing a strong faith foundation to CN village Christians through Christian nurture.

On 16th September 1944 Sawday breathed his last. He had become very fragile and bedridden for some time. The life of a legendary missionary, a great church planter and builder par excellent, thus came to an end. He was 90 years old.

As the news of his death spread, thousands of people, cutting across religions, thronged to pay him the last respect. There was a great concourse of people at his funeral. The body was carried by people who were redeemed from slavery by Sawday, taken in procession in the streets of Mysore and was buried. A great era of Mission work thus came to an end.

Further progress in Talwadi region

Besides Kottanahalli, where baptisms had taken place in 1943, in a few more inaccessible places also congregations were established. In 1946 as many as 46 people were prepared for baptism in **Panakanahalli.** Likewise, in Singanpura 21 adults took baptism in1947 and thus the tiny congregation there grew further in strength.

All those villages i.e. Karalavadi, Kottanahalli, Singanapura and Panakahalli which as already noted, were all part of a very backward region infested with malaria, leprosy and so on as well as wild life. Missionaries were certainly rejoiced much at the establishment of new congregations in these unreached places of southern part of CN taluk, in the border area with the Tamil country. Hill, the senior missionary in charge of both Mysore and CN circuits explained the accession of new congregations with satisfaction exclaimed "No mass movement yet in Mysore, but still movement and still progress" (MDR, 1946, p.8).

Educational and community health work in Talwadi region

The Mission opened quite a few schools in its new field, namely Talwadi region. That included in Talwadi, Panakahalli and Karlavadi. Mission also started intensive leprosy treatment and eradication programme in Tiganare and surrounding villages. It was in Tiganare, a very backward place of Talwadi region, Dr. Abraham of Hadya Mission hospital, succumbed to malaria, while working among the leprosy patients.

Second round of baptisms in Mudnakod, Masgapura and Kiragsura

As if to crown the series of conversions which was taking place, in 1946 51 people were baptized in Mudnakod, a village within CN, on the south western side, where first baptisms had taken place as early as in 1936. In 1945 twenty-five people were baptized in Masgapura, where first baptisms had taken place in 1920. Earlier in 1942 Kiragsur, a village closure to Kastur, also witnessed several baptisms enabling the little congregation to swell in numbers. It was way back in 1910 and in 1915 just 2-3 families had joined the Christian fold in that village (MDR, 1942, p.9).

Lay people-The prime church planters

A very remarkable feature in the growth of village churches in CN area was the active role played by lay members of the church. It was mainly those lay people, ordinary men and women of little or no education and a people of very little or no means of their own, who became the prime church planters in the area! The distinguished feature of growth of the churches in CN area and the vital part of neo converts in it was explained in a Mission report in 1933, which was the Silver Jubilee year of Kastur church/movement:

"It (Gospel) has spread, not as we could have worked for convenience in oversight, but along the tangled path of outcaste family relationships and marriage connections, as those who had seen the light spoke of it to those whom they met in the course of their work or their social life" (MDR,1933,p.4).

In 1937 the missionary report lucidly states how the church planting was carried on with lay people/ neo converts actively partaking in it. It was reported: 'entire area is surveyed and relations of converts living in different villages identified and visited. Evangelists and relatives regularly visit them' (MDR, 1937, p17). More about lay leaders role is noted separately, in Chapter VII.

The dream of planting churches in western villages remained unfulfilled

Missionaries always nurtured a dream of planting churches in villages west of Nanjanagudu-Chamarajanagara road. Western side was seen with fascination and considered as a fertile ground for Gospel. Missionaries even dreamt that when the western villages filled with churches Heggawadi would be the centre of Mission work and not Kastur which lies to the east of the triangle. They rejoiced when Kerehalli (1923), Heggewadi (1931) and Bedarapura (1935) churches were founded hoping that it was beginning of a great expansion in western villages. Later Mudnakod church was founded in1936 but no further success gained and the long-cherished dream of the missionaries remained almost unrealized (Statement of Mysore District Policy, 1936 p.3).

CN villages and the year on which first baptism(s) took place there

1.	CN town	1885
2.	Kastur	1908
3.	Bhogapura	1908
4.	Mangala Hosur	1909
5.	HoHomma	1910
6.	Doddarayanapet	1910
7.	Kiragsur	1910
8.	Madigahalli	1914
9.	Singonapura	1915
10.	Honnalli	1916
11.	Kallalli	1916
12.	Masgapura	1917
13.	Hardya (Hadya)	1922
14.	Kirugunda	1923
15.	Kerehalli	1923
16.	Kellamballi	1924
17.	Annalli	1924
18.	Bisselwadi	1927
19.	Basvatti	1929

20.	Ummathur	1931
21.	ugani	1931
22.	Heggewadi	1931
23.	Kamaravadi	1932
24.	Dodda Homma	1933
25.	Andakalli	1934
26.	Bedarapura	1935
27.	Kuderu	1936
28.	Deshavalli	1936
29.	Kalkunda	1936
30.	Mudnakod	1936
31.	Ankusha Rayana Pura	1938
32.	Metluvadi	1940
33.	Singonapura(T)	1940
34.	Tiganare	1942
35.	T.Gajanur	1943
36.	T.Hosur	1943
37.	Karalavadi	1943
38.	Kottanahalli	1943
39.	Dodda Gajanur	1944
40.	Panakahalli	1946

(Source: Register of Adult Baptism, Wesleyan Mission, CN Circuit)

First Evangelists of main congregations in CN villages

C.N Town	Bhakti Siromani	1885
Kastur	J.L.Jonathan	1908
Bhogapura	C.George	1908
M.Hosur	D.Mark	1909
Homma	R.Kenchappa	1910
Madigahalli	A Shiromani	1914
Masgapura	Samuel Sadhu	1919
Hadya	R.Kenchappa	1922
Kirugunda	Clement Caleb	1923
Kerehalli	R.Kenchappa	1923
Kellamballi	M.P.Soans	1924
Basavatti	S.Chintamani	1929
Ugani	C.Eliappa	1931
Mudnakod	C. Yohana	1936
Mettluvadi	H.B.Dehalo	1940
Tiganare	S.Samuel	1943
Gajanur	S. Sunderraj	1943
Dodda Gajanur	M.K.Arnold	1944
Karalavadi	S.Krupedas	1944
Panakahalli	H. B. Dehalo	1945

(Source: Wesleyan Mission Annual Reports/MDRs)

Note

1. From 1908 to 1932 most of the Baptisms were officiated by Sawday.

2. The baptismal register preserved at CN town church (Tomlinson Memorial church) 'Register of Adult Baptisms' is a historic document, wherein Sawday began registering the details of baptized candidates.

3. It may be noted that Hadya and Kirugunda are not part of CN taluk/district. In civil administration both those places belong to Nanjanagud taluk and part of Mysore district. Even in the church administration they now belong to Mysore Area and not to CN Area. However, when the Wesleyan Mission started working, both those villages namely Hadya and Kirugunda were very much part and parcel of CN region and in a way, even now, culturally.

Few basic and distinct features of origin and growth of CN village churches

1. It was Panchamas, a people who were from time unknown subjected to a life of most inhuman oppression, yearned to embrace Christian faith. They were groaning and yearning for liberation, freedom and dignity. The desire to learn about new God, desire for social betterment, desire for education all those factors played a role. Their conversion to Christian faith was an 'exodus' or a strenuous journey for liberation. In other words, it was a revolt against the age-old caste oppression on them.

2. The new believers experienced an inexplicable joy and solace in the new faith and the community they had willingly/ voluntarily embraced. Gospel made a deep appeal on them

(Goadie, 1936, p.65). Ignorant people they were but they experienced a great joy for the new faith (MDR, 19111, pp. 41-42). The Good News was a 'Joyful News' for them! They very much cherished to be part of the new faith community come what may,be it persecution, harassment, droughts or pestilence.

3. Their contentment in the new faith was unquestionable and it was amply manifested in an amazing and over flowing missionary spirit which they always carried. They were very eager that every kith and kin of theirs should be received into the Christian fold.

4. The entire Wesleyan Mission period (1885-1947) in CN villages was a highly turbulent time. The period saw two World Wars, global economic depression, Freedom Struggle in India, recurring communal riots, growing anti-Christian Mission agitations and so on. Adding, there was chronic and recurring drought and pestilence. However, the missionaries continued un deterred; so also, were the newly converted.

5. Those who decided to join the Christian faith were aware, in advance, that only further troubles by way of harassment and persecution were waiting for them. Their conversion to new faith was far from proselytism or rice Christianity.

6. Despite a very phenomenal work carried on in CN villages, with many people joining Christian fold, it was not a mass movement. Even from the depressed class communities as a rule no such response to the Gospel, only a small segment had embraced Christian faith, a fact which quite disappointed the missionaries.

7. Pastoral care which was well organized and vigilant was the strong foundation underneath the growth of the churches and

the spread of the Good News in CN villages. The pastoral care which provided was spiritually nurturing. The Christian nurture which they provided helped people effectively to inculcate and develop a Christian character resulting in a visible change/transformation in their life, a fact often testified even by non-Christian villagers.

8. A very distinct feature Of Wesleyan Mission/ Sawday's work was that the children and youth were given top priority. Sawday had once stated: 'Hope of the Church is in children and young people whom God has entrusted to our care' (MDR, 1920, P. 68). The educational endeavors, redemption of scores of children in slavery and vocational training imparted were few examples to the top priority they had given to children, youth and women.

9. The Christian witness as well as pastoral care was not limited to internal spirituality alone. Along with spiritual nurture the missionaries did everything to empower the new community through educational, medical, industrial/vocational training, literature and through several other short and long term innovative programmes. Further it was most important that they gave a prime priority to empower women folk. Indeed, their endeavors were truly liberative and wholistic.

CHAPTER – 5

From an Endless Social Oppression: Moving Towards Liberation

The movement which began in Kastur village in 1908 and soon spread to surrounding villages of CN area was phenomenal, in more than one way. The 'Kastur Movement' as it was then known in Mission circles raised ripples far beyond CN area and Mysore province. It was something like an unexpected rainfall and a bounty harvest after a long spell of drought! Although it was not a mass movement nevertheless it was a 'movement' towards Christian faith that was taking place in several CN villages beginning from Kastur.

The neo converts were all exclusively from Panchama community, a people who from time unknown were chained as victims of caste oppression. Apart from abject poverty and illiteracy they were also victims of, yet another vicious practice named jitha (bonded labour), which had made a large number of them as slaves to upper caste landlords/moneylenders.

The dreadful and dehumanized socio-economic condition in which they were living must had compelled them to make a final decision to embrace Christian faith. They saw a beacon of hope and solace in it (MDR, 1919, pp.67-68). It was that hope that led them towards an unflinching faith in Jesus Christ as the only savior and the liberator (Ibid, p.50).

A people groaning under the heavy yoke of caste

The people who began responding to the call of the Gospel in CN villages were exclusively from Holeya social origin. Holeyas were, and even now, the largest community among the depressed class people in the region. Except a miniscule minority almost all the Holeya families were landless, living in abject poverty and illiteracy, ignorance and superstition.

Like all other depressed class people, Holeyas too used to shed their blood and sweat as serfs and servants in the fields and in the backyards of the homes of the dominant caste people. Majority of Holeyas were labourers and slaves. Their lives solely depended on Lingayat and Gowda land lords.

The worst fact was that many them were working for their masters for life long as bonded labourers or as slaves. The irony was that it was their labour, which was substantially contributing to the village economy as well as of their land lords, and it was their scavenging labour which was keeping the villages clean. However, for all the service they rendered and shedding of blood and sweat, they were being treated as mere scum or trash. They were treated as ritually polluted, therefore considered 'untouchables'. With caste becoming accepted social norm with legitimization by religion injustice was institutionalized. The untouchables became a debased, brutalized and dehumanized section of the population. The caste as a socio religious system had totally succeeded in reducing them a socially degraded, economically disabled and politically voiceless people.

The missionaries observed the pernicious caste system and they were quick to discover its multifarious manifestations in Mysore province, including in CN area. Certainly, their encounter with caste was an exhausting experience for them.

Missionaries' encounter with caste --experiences and perceptions

- Holeyas (as well as other untouchables) live in separate isolated keris outside or on the periphery of villages. They live ostracized with little or no social interaction with the rest of the villagers or caste Hindus.

- No caste Hindu will ever enter Holeya residential locality since it was believed to be ritually polluting and repulsive.

- If at all Holeyas, on some errands, have to enter caste Hindu streets in village they should take of their footwear and walk in bare feet only.

- In the street if an upper caste person comes walking across, Holeya should leap sideways and stand head bent (Thompson, p.176).

- A Holeya should not ever learn to read or write. Missionaries saw that whenever they admitted Dalit children to school there were huge protests (MDR, 1932, p.2).

- He should not read sacred books lest his tongue would be cut (ibid).

- Holeyas should not draw water from village wells. While Muslims were allowed to draw water from village wells Holeyas or Christian converts were not allowed.

- Holeyas have to walk long way to collect water from a pond or stream outside the village. This is specially during summer and drought spells. Water thus collected was not potable water and therefore people easily succumb to various water borne diseases.

- Holeyas should not wear a dress below his knee (ibid).

- They should not enter village tea shop but stand at the entrance.

- They should not stand or sit in public places like village *chavadi* /platform or in bus stand etc.

- They were not being rendered service by village barbers, washer men, tailors and other village functionaries.

- They may buy things in shop, but only after caste Hindus finished with their buying.

- Holeya children were made to sit separately in the schools.

- Holeyas should be readily available to do all kinds of menial work and errands, including scavenging, carrying carcasses and so on, at anytime of the day or night.

- Holeyas were once land owners and cultivators but upper castes had subdued them. Due to debt trap a large number of Holeyas including children were forced to become bonded labourers or slaves, lifelong. Once Holeyas were thrifty farmers but they fell into slavery.

- A small number of Holeya families owned some lands, but mostly dry lands, which were of little use. Further the biting poverty forced many of them to even mortgage their precious piece of land.

- Apart from agricultural coolie work Holeyas were also found as village watchmen, water bailiffs and so on. Their opinion was often sought whenever village surveys were undertaken.

- A subdued culture has become a part very much of their personality or behavior.

Atrocities were being committed on Holeyas, regularly. In fact, they were a very common occurrence in their life, about which none paid any notice (Ibid p.176). They were treated like animals, in inhuman ways as *persona non grata* and abused verbally and physically. They were a people deprived of justice, freedom and human dignity.

The missionaries found the living condition of Holeyas as inexplicably deplorable. Their encounter with caste was a strange and complex experience. They saw the condition of Dalits as totally dehumanized and debased. One of the earliest and very descriptive articles on caste was written by Mysore–based missionary E.J. Hardey in 1852 (MDR, 1852, pp.11-17).

Missionaries uncompromising opposition against caste

Right from the beginning of their work in CN area as well as in rest of Mysore province the Wesleyan Mission took a bold and an uncompromising position opposing caste. Their position on caste may be briefly summarized as follows:

Caste is antithetical to Gospel

Caste is totally antithetical or opposite to Gospel / Christian faith. Gospel liberates and unites people, where as caste divides them and subjugates. Therefore, no compromise should be ever made with caste or any of caste practices, at any cost.

Untouchability- the obnoxious and evil outcome of caste

Caste and its major evil fallout namely untouchablity are part and parcel of Hindu religion.

Religion has sanctioned and legitimized caste

By giving religious sanction to caste Hindu religion has legitimized/ institutionalized injustice.

Caste is integral part of Hindu religion

Caste was intrinsically related to Hindu religion, as part and parcel of it. Thus, religion approved an unjust and oppressive social evil/ system. This should not be supported at any cost. The missionaries conceded that England too had terrible customs a hundred years ago. But only difference was, in India all the inhuman customs intimately connected with religion. (MDR,1921, p.8).

Caste is the greatest obstacle to missionary work

Missionaries perceived caste as the 'monster evil' and the biggest obstacle, insurmountable difficulty to missionary work (MDR, 1852, p.11, 1853, pp.11-17). Due to family bond which was closely intertwined to caste, people were unable to come forward to take baptism, although most, especially youth, appeared to be fully convinced of the Gospel truth, and the bankruptcy of Hindu religion (MDR,1919, p.66).

Caste a big obstacle to progress of the land and people

Caste was the great obstacle to the progress or development of people and land.

Caste has infiltrated in to all religions

Missionaries saw that caste was all pervasive in all religious communities. Missionary Hardy in his elaborate article in 1852 had noted that in Mysore, Hindu religion had 486 caste groups; Papists (Roman Catholics) had 70 castes, Muslims 86, and Dalits 200 castes or sub castes, within themselves (Hardy, in MDR, 1852, p.13).

British rulers, though they are Christians, support caste and idolatry

British rulers of India have shown a patronizing policy on caste and idolatry (MDR, 1852, P.12). British rulers had tended to patronize idolatry to get revenue (MDR, 1921, p.8)! The Circar (British India government) indirectly supports caste; no way it destroys the distinctions (MDR, 1853, P.12). For the missionaries such a policy was unfortunate and unacceptable. As 'Christian' rulers British government had a responsibility to eradicate caste, but instead they were promoting and patronizing it. Sawday stated Christian nation is ruling millions. Its duty to proclaim salvation (MDR,1895, p.1). The missionaries strong criticism on British rulers in this matter was expressed most of the times (MDR, 1915, p.1, also 1921, p.8). The missionaries also criticized the British government for not abolishing Disability Act in Mysore province (MDR, 1921, p.36). This oppressive Act deprived the converts the right of inheritance. Indirectly it deprived depressed class people their right of freedom of religion.

Roman Catholic churches condone/accommodate caste

Roman Catholic church condoned/ approved of caste which Wesleyan missionaries felt very deplorable. Catholic policy of compromising with caste was strongly criticized. Missionaries contested that the Roman Catholic number grows faster because they compromise with one and all! Missionaries stated: 'While Protestant Missions strike at the root of caste and idolatry, the Roman Catholics sanction both, and will by this means quickly grow into a Multitude' (MDR, 1850, p.8).

Mysore is very religious and conservative

Mysore province, especially Mysore city was very religious and a centre of conservative religion and bigotry. In fact, Mysore was seen as 'a gutter of ideology' (MDR.1878, p.30, also Thompson, p.176). Missionaries believed that the Brahmins dominate because they were enjoying the Royal support. Under this condition, obviously, caste and superstitions thrived (MDR, 1861, p.20).

Missionaries believed that it was Christian Mission work which triggered reform within Hindu society

Missionaries saw that an increasing number of educated upper caste Hindus had started showing repulsion towards caste. They even noticed how an increasing number of educated Hindus showing concern to 'uplift' depressed class people. Missionaries contested that this new concern which was developing among educated Hindus was primarily because of Mission school teaching and a spirit of reform which the missionaries triggered within Hinduism (MDR, 1906; MDR, 1913, p.44; MDR, 1912, p.35). 'We believe we may safely claim this movement the outcome of our work' stated the missionaries (MDR,1913,p.44).

Hindus and Muslims cannot uplift depress class people

However, the missionaries also strongly contested that Hindus and Muslims cannot really uplift the depressed class people. It was stated, "neither Hinduism nor muhammadanism has the power that is needed. Much of the missionary enthusiasm of Hinduism is based not on love of the outcaste, but on hate of the Christians" (MDR, 1923, p.9). Educated Hindus recent concern for the depressed class people was not genuine. Missionaries held that the newly showing up concern of some educated Hindus towards depressed class people was only a ploy to obstruct Christian Mission work among those people (Ibid, p.9).

Brahmins are main promoters of caste

Missionaries observed that the Hindu Orthodoxy/Brahmin segment among the Hindu population was the prime promoter of caste and carried a great deal of contempt against anyone including Christian Mission who tried to oppose the old social order. They first used to ignore the conversion of those hapless, but soon became alert at its magnitude and its consequences to themselves (Thompson, p.202). Missionaries saw it ironical that although the upper caste people were the maximum beneficiaries of Mission institutions, especially schools, they were the people who held missionaries in greatest contempt trying to harass them, endlessly. In English School (later named as Hardwicke school) in Mysore for example out of 156 students in 1856, 95 were Brahmins, and the rest belonged to 14 other communities. Likewise in one of the first Mission schools in CN town out of 18 students 15 were Brahmins (MDR, 1889, pp. xxii-xxiii)

Brahmins Pharisaical, whereas depress class people are debased

Missionaries perceived Brahmins as pharisaical and the pariahs (Dalits) as debased (MDR, 1890, p.3).

Even the depressed class people practice caste–they have hierarchy within their communities

Missionaries saw that ironically the divisive caste had infiltrated into the culture of depressed class people too. They saw hierarchy and practice of untouchability even among the depressed classes.

Examples of a few good understanding/gestures of caste Hindus towards Christians

While a general contempt of caste Hindus towards Dalits/ Dalit converts to Christianity appeared to be very common, missionary reports have also recorded a few cases of rare caste Hindu gestures which appeared like crossing the parochial and casteist lines. Here are few such instances:

Firstly, the one that took place in Kastur in 1912. The 'mother church' in Kastur formed in 1908 had for quite some time no proper place for worship and for the residence of its evangelist. Mission reports states that at that juncture a caste Hindu man gave a site, followed by two other caste men also volunteering to give some land for the purpose (HF, 1923, p.35). The land thus given was a good ideal site. It was located between caste Hindu and Dalit localities. Soon the Mission built a spacious thatched prayer shed and a pastor's house in that land.

Secondly, the congregation which was formed in Bhogapura, a village adjacent to Kastur had no proper place to worship for about 3-4 years. The small flock were worshipping in one room which was also pastor's house and a school. It was at this juncture a Brahmin headman in the village gave half of his house to Christians (MDR, 1912, p.37). Sawday had vividly explained the joy of the little flock of securing a place of worship of their own, 'The joy of the people may be imagined. They had rarely been allowed to approach the place, for their very shadow meant pollution, and now to think it belonged to them or at least to the Mission' (ibid).

Instances of human kindness or gestures, crossing caste or religious barriers were not too rare. The missionaries recognized them and had not forgotten to briefly report about such instances with an openness of mind. One such instance was in 1928 when the villages of CN area were ravaged by a prolonged drought for 5 years. Human misery, also of livestock, was beyond description. Missionaries were trying their best to help people, but the crisis was too enormous for them to handle. It was under this condition the Missionaries reported of a striking act of human kindness. The missionaries reported, 'A Christ-like caste man gifted a piece of land in low-lying area, where Christians dug a well and got water' (MDR, 1928, p.58).

When the Mission was planning to build a chapel in Hadya, a 'good man' offered land. However, that rare gesture could not be realized. The generous caste Hindu who offered to donate land for the construction of the chapel became a target of a few villagers, hatred and a big problem followed (MDR, 1929, p.54).

An incident that was epic which took place in Mandya on the day of conversion of 64 persons in 1924 is worth noting. When there was a great commotion in the town against Baptisms,it was the wise words of a caste Hindu lawyer which made the agitators finally calm down. It was reported that the lawyer told the agitating crowd, 'If the people really desire to become Christians, why should we prevent them? They have perfect right, like the rest of us, to please themselves' (MDR,1924,59). Today there is a flourishing congregation in Mandya.

Missionary crusade against caste 'within' and 'without'

The Wesleyan missionaries who were totally disposed against caste fought against it tirelessly, within the young congregations as well as in the society at large. Indeed, it was a crusade against caste.

Struggle against caste within the young congregations

Preaching, teaching and corporate worship to nurture the neo converts in Christian values and character were the primary instrument through which missionaries fought against caste from 'within'. They were perceived as effective antidote against the deep-rooted caste culture. Missionaries were well aware that the task of eradicating casteist and heathen practices and beliefs among the first-generation Christians was not easy. Missionaries also observed with dismay how the Mysore city Christians sometimes tend to look down Christians from Kastur villages as inferior to others (MDR, 1922, p.5). Missionaries were indeed very unhappy about that 'looking down'/discriminating attitude by anyone including within Christian fold. They strongly dissented casteist attitude and practices within the churches. It was their firm belief that preaching, and teaching and a vigilant pastoral care were the only way to effectively combat obnoxious caste/casteism within the new community. It was missionary Tomlinson who played a very important role in strengthening and promoting Christian nurture in the young congregations of CN villages that played an important part in nurturing the neo converts in a Christian culture. Pastoral house visits, Cottage prayer meetings, evening prayers in the church and in the families, Bible studies, Women's Fellowship, Youth Fellowship and community elders' meetings became a regular feature which greatly helped to inculcate and promote a new culture, as opposed to caste culture.

Remarkable Role of mission schools, boarding homes in eradicating caste

Boarding schools, orphanages, vocational training centre, hospitals/ dispensaries and such other Mission institutions, where caste had absolutely no place at all, became very effective catalytic instruments in dispelling caste and promoting a new culture among the neo converts (MDR.1919, p. 5). Among all, the boarding schools remained invaluable institution in molding young people in a culture different to caste culture (ref. Thompson, 196; Goudie,,1936,p.66 and Statement Mysore District Policy,1936,p.4). Pointing to the invaluable role of boarding homes a missionary exclaimed,'There lies the hope and promise of the future.' (Ibid)Wilson referring to the missionaries' anti-caste stance taken up in Mission schools stated: 'Our great principle seems to have been settled as soon as educational work begun, the principle that in Christian schools, differences of caste could not be recognized. From the beginning caste was seen as a negative aspect and not as a characteristic of Christianity (Wilson H.S, *Wesleyan Kanarese Mission in the Mysore Territory*, ICH Review, June 1986, p.64, referring MDR, 1921, p.29).

The Mission institutions sent a very clear message to the society at large disapproving caste, absolutely and totally. Obviously, in each of those Mission institutions, especially schools, boarding homes and hospitals, where missionaries stood uncompromisingly against caste, they had to face a great deal of opposition, especially in the initial several years of Mission work. However, the missionaries continued their crusade against caste undeterred, without succumbing to any pressure. All their actions sent a powerful message to the neo converts as well as to the general public that they were not going to recognize caste, and not going to compromise in this matter, at any cost.

Anger of Hindu orthodoxy on missionaries' anti-caste stance

It was understandably from the Hindu orthodoxy the missionaries had to face most bitter opposition in their struggle against caste. When the Mission admitted backward class and depressed class pupils in Mission schools and when non-Brahmin teachers were being appointed as teachers in Mission schools the Hindu orthodoxy used to cry foul. In many cases they used to threaten boycotting the school(s). Same caste Hindu dissent was shown in Mission hospitals and dispensaries also during the initial several years. However, the missionaries remained unwavering and uncompromising in their anti-caste or in their equality of all people policy.

Missionaries campaign against the oppressive 'Disability Act'

There was a law in Mysore province since quite a long time according to which if a person converts to other religion, he/she loses all rights to ancestral property, including even on their wives and own children (MDR,1905, p.ii; MDR, 1930, p.13). This strange and oppressive law indirectly denied the depressed class people their very right to freedom of religion. It fortified caste and placed a strong obstacle against peoples' conversion. Such a law did not exist in other states in India which were directly ruled by the British but it existed in states like Mysore province which were not directly ruled by the British. Therefore, the missionaries had to wage a long-drawn crusade against that arbitrary and oppressive law. The missionaries did not even fail to strongly criticize the 'Christian' British government, which according to them was not doing anything to remove the Disability Act (MDR, 1921, p.32-33). They saw that the Disability Act stood as the biggest hurdle for anyone who wanted to join Christian faith. The anti- missionary elements very often used to scare the gullible enquirers how they would lose property and everything else if they get converted.

It goes to the credit of Wesleyan missionaries that they consistently and strongly lobbied against Disability law, almost from the beginning of 20th century. In 1909 together with Roman Catholic and LMS representatives they met Maharaja and submitted an appeal to revoke the Act (MDR, 1909, p. ix; 1910, p.xiv). Quintessence of their appeal was: 'give justice just as British ruled states' (HF, 1909, p.204). Maharaja had an open mind on the whole issue and made a positive assurance to the Christian delegation. However, it was ironical that not only Hindus but also Muslim representatives in the State Council vehemently opposed any change or revocation of the old law (MDR, 1905, p.11). Therefore the missionaries had to continue their campaign against the oppressive law for a longer and indefinite time. However, it was only at the eve of Independence the matter was finally set right and the obstacle was cleared.

Rampant prevalence of Jitha/Slavery

A highly oppressive socio-economic practice which the missionaries found extensively in CN area was jitha which was nothing but slavery. Although this practice was found in many parts of Mysore province, it was in the chronically drought-stricken regions like CN area that was most rampant. The overwhelming majority of people enslaved in jitha were of depressed class origin and some from very backward Shudra communities. jitha was intrinsically related to caste and it was mostly the vulnerable depressed classes who were being entrapped into this slavery which made their life inexplicably miserable.

As the Christ-ward movement which began in Kastur and eventually spread to many surrounding villages the missionaries discovered that not only adults but also children, as young as of four years, were entrapped in jitha. To his great shock Sawday discovered that even in many converted families their children even of very tender age were chained to slavery. It was this sight of children being entrapped in the inhumane jitha system which deeply disturbed Sawday and forced him to work on liberating those children (H.F.1921, p 317). Sawday stated in 1921, 'It touched me greatly to see the faces of the lads who have been sold into serfdom, and what all costs be redeemed if they are to learn anything of Christ or to be of any value to the church' (H.F. 1921, p.317).

Sawday was then based in Mysore city as superintendent of both Mysore and CN circuits. It was during this time i.e. first quarter of 20th century he did an astounding work of redeeming scores of children in CN villages from the chains of slavery and set them free.

Debt trap-the root cause of jitha

The overwhelming majority of the depressed class people in that period were living in abject, nay absolute poverty. Usually illness, marriages in the family or some unforeseen/ emergencies would force them to borrow from their village landlords/ money lenders. The amount they borrow was on compound interest with an interest rate ranging from 30% to 50% per month, at times even more! The exorbitant interest amount grows in leaps and bounds, day after day and it becomes practically impossible for the poor borrower to pay back even the interest amount, leave alone the principal amount. While the interest amount escalates sky high, the money lender becomes more and more aggressive in his demands. In this circumstance the condition of the borrower becomes vulnerable, a total wreck. This situation first forces the borrower to sell of his piece of land, if he has any, to the money lender, usually for a song. The missionaries reported that "the problem of paying the interest and getting back the field is apparently insoluble that the people lose hearts, and then lose houses, field and everything. Crushing burden of interest would break their heart and ruin their home" (Goudie, p.63). It was while he was being caught up in this helpless situation, the borrower pledges his child/children to money lender as bonded labourers or slaves (Thompson...p.178). From that day onwards, those children pledged on jitha become property of the moneylender land lord. Missionaries reporting the helpless condition of those in debt trap stated, "caught with money lender, from whose clutches they tried to extricate themselves as vainly as fly from the meshes of web'" (MDR, 1909, p.38).

Once a child is sold to jitha in lieu of the debt made, the child becomes a property of its master. A life of inexplicably dehumanized slavery with no escape from it begins and continues till the end of life. Jitha child was given an old rugged blanket, a stick, put up in a dirty stable and provided with leftover food to eat. Cow herding, scavenging and such other work become his main job in the initial years. However, soon he is being 'promoted' into, nay forced into hard labour. He gets nothing as wage for his labour day and night, but all his labour is supposedly in lieu of settling the endless interest accrued for the little amount his parents had borrowed from the money lender land lord. A jitha child is deprived of everything, be it parental care, schooling, in fact he/she loses very childhood and a normal human life. They are also subjected to unlimited cruelty and domesticated as slaves of their master, for life.

Sawday's monumental work of redeeming scores of slave children

The miserable condition of those who were in jitha especially of children deeply moved Sawday. To a person like Sawday, who by nature had a very affectionate heart towards children, the sight of suffering slave children deeply disturbed him. He recollected how way back during his tenure in Tumkur (1876-1894) he had rescued a number of children from jitha, which had helped them in finding a new lease of life. He remembered how some of those former slave children were now serving as evangelists. It was his greatest joy. Sargant states how by 1940s the ex-jitha boys had become capable evangelists (Sargant, p.11).

Now, in CN area Sawday was greatly disturbed when he saw a vast number of children entrapped as slaves and suffering endlessly. He lamented 'My heart bleeds for those lads sold to slavery! O, poverty! In poor families 2-3 are slave boys or young men. It is terrible .. . . (H.F., 1921, p.318). Soon after the conversions began taking place in 1908 in Kastur and in its neighboring villages Sawday plunged into the indomitable task of rescuing children from jitha. It was indeed a great 'mission liberation'! However, it required large amount of money to redeem the children. But, a determined Sawday never gave up or looked back. By 1909 i.e., within a year the first conversions began to take place in Kastur village where he redeemed eight children from slavery. He started making earnest appeal to his friends and well wishers in England and in India to generously contribute 'redemption' amount to rescue children in slavery. The response was over whelming.

A report of Sawday in 1910 vividly shows his deep concern for slave children and how he used to passionately appeal for support, "It was delightful to hear them and to realize what the love of Christ had done for these little ones. If our friends in England could only see them.... The beautiful work in the redemption of the children. The work is glorious, the opportunity is unique, the need is great and urgent, and gifts for the uplifting of the adults and the redemption of the children will be most gratefully received by Mr. Sawday in Mysore city" (MDR, 1910, p.34).

Sargant had noted how Sawday had an 'amazing gift for writing' making passionate appeals to people which would touch the hearts of the prospective donors (Sargant, p.29 also MDR, 1929, pp.51-55). Sawday fully utilized this skill of writing appeal throughout his five decades of missionary work, in India, first in Tumkur area and later for a long period in Mysore region.

Sawday always experienced a great joy and sense of fulfillment in redeeming children. He once exclaimed:

> "No part of our work has given us more joy than the redemption of those children from lifelong slavery" (Harvest Field, 1910, p.).

The guiding principle behind Sawday's mission of redeeming children in slavery

The guiding principle behind sawday's remarkable work in redeeming slave children lies in his faith perception. In a report, sawday stated it as follows: 'They (children) must be slaves of neither man nor cruel social system, but of the Lord Jesus only. To speak to such men of a Savior who has a message for their souls only, but who has no word to cheer them in facing the bitter sorrow of their everyday life and grinding poverty seems somewhat of a mockery' (MDR,1919, p.68).

Few selected cases of Redemption of Children

Three children redeemed in Kastur, 1908

This appears to be the first case of jitha redemption in CN area for which Sawday was instrumental. The newly converted family in Kastur had three children sold to slavery. They were in the age group of 13, 10, and 9-year-old girl with no chance of redeeming themselves from the slavery. The local evangelist Jonathan was very keen that all the three children of this newly converted family be redeemed. He was persistently pleading with Sawday to redeem them. However, the redemption of those three children required a large amount Rs.75/ (five pounds). Without any further delay Sawday appealed to some friends in Mysore to kindly help. In no time the required amount was contributed by a well-wisher and all the three children were redeemed.

Two children redeemed in Bhogapura – 1909

Bhogapura is a village adjacent to Kastur. The case was related to a newly converted family, the second family to be converted to Christian faith in this village. The family had four children. Out of this the older one was a blind young man and other two were sold as slaves to caste Hindu land lord. Since the debt which the family had made was increasing due to the exorbitant interest, the land lord started demanding to give him the third child (a girl) also as a slave. Sawday arranged for the redemption money and the two boys were finally redeemed. The girl was sent to the boarding school in Mysore and the two boys who were redeemed were sent to Tumkur orphanage.

Three children redeemed in M. Hosur, 1914

This family consisted of a widow mother and five children. Three children were working for a caste Hindu land lord as slaves. Hoping that some kind-hearted friend will support

Sawday redeemed three children by paying Rs.75/.

A boy redeemed in Singonapura, 1918

Singonapura, a village situated north of CN town. A family had joined the Christian fold, but the bright looking boy of the family was in slavery. Sawday appealed to his friends for their helping hand. A family in Woodford, England contributed the ransom amount in memory of their son who had died in war. The slave boy was redeemed.

Three boys were redeemed in M. Hosur -1919

The widow in M. Hosur, Bhagyamma had one daughter and three sons. All the three boys were working as slaves. Sawday redeemed the three boys and sent them to Tumkur orphanage.

Eighteen years old young man redeemed, Kastur, 1919

A young lad of 18 years of a newly converted family in Kastur was working as slave. The boy was looking very bright and promising. A friend of Sawday in London contributed the ransom amount and the boy was set free.

The above noted cases are only few examples for reference. During his long period of service Sawday had rescued scores of children from jitha. The Harvest Field acknowledged this in 1919 stating, "Much work is done for the social uplifting of depressed classes. Mr. Sawday has been instrumental in saving scores of lads who have been forced to live in jitha, a form of slavery." (HF, 1919,p. 184).

In the laborious task of arranging for redemption amount, Sawday often depended on the kindness of his friends and well-wishers in England as well as in India. Scores of friends responded to Sawday's appeal which made the redemption of a very large number of slave children possible. In some emergency circumstances Sawday had to use the District Loan Fund of the Mission.

'Jholam Fund' - a self help initiative to redeem slave children

Further it is striking that Sawday also encouraged the young congregations of CN villages to raise funds locally to pay for the redemption of slave children among them. The "Jholam Fund" (maize fund) was one such indigenous initiative which was tried in Kastur and other villages of CN area as a self-help effort to redeem their children from slavery.

A report of 1938 reveals how a person, who was once a slave boy, donated a sum to get released a jitha boy (MDR, 1938, p.23).

Educating people against the evil of jitha

Besides redeeming the slave children and rehabilitating them Sawday used to educate people not to initiate their children into jitha. He did this as social awareness, whenever there was opportunity, be it in preaching, teaching or in conversations with people. It was reported how Sawday, once while addressing a gathering, made to stand a jitha redeemed girl and a boy on a table. Pointing to the bright physical appearance and clean dress of those two children and comparing them to the debased condition of children in jitha, Sawday demonstrated the transformation or the tangible result that could take place in a child's life after redemption (HF, 1918, p.267).

Visit of the Synod Commission – Recommendations on jitha

A Synod Commission of the Wesleyan Mission made an inspection visit to Mysore province, including CN village congregations in 1941. It was a 10-member Commission comprising of men and women. The Commission recognized the Christ ward movement which was in progress in CN villages as a 'Community Movement' and it was phenomenal.

Among the many important observations, the Commission had made its recommendations on jitha were striking. The Commission noted that jitha was 'pledging service of children to land holders instead of cash payment of interest on loan received by the parents' (MDR.1941, p 33). The Commission observed that among the harmful effects included deprival of school, worship and Sunday school for slave children. It was also underlined that the system was a serious obstacle to the growth of the church.

The Commission appreciated Sawday's commitment and efforts in redeeming children from jitha. It observed that while such efforts should be continued caution should be taken that it was not proselytism. Further the Commission observed that people should raise money themselves to redeem jitha children among them. Using of District Fund for the redemption of jitha may be avoided. Three important suggestions of the Commission may be noted:

1. Start a campaign against jitha, irrespective of religion. Appeal and lobby with the Government for its eradication. Promote public awareness against jitha.

2. Spiritual deliverance should stand first. Only this provides perspective to the struggle against jitha.

3. In fighting against jitha educate people to self help.

"I Owe Only to Christ!"- An interesting witness

Sawday's pioneer work in redeeming scores of children in jitha was a remarkable saga of faith and Christian witness. It was a great story of transformation: Once slaves of oppressive moneylender landlords, liberated, and now becoming slaves of Christ! An interesting story may be briefly noted here as a befitting witness to the transformation: A young man who was once a slave boy and redeemed by Sawday got educated and trained to be a teacher. Since he had a desire to serve the church as a full-time evangelist/pastor he stood before the Provincial Synod for an interview. This was sometime around the year 1938. The interview was to decide about his selection for the ministerial training. The committee asked the customary question to the young man, 'Are you in debt?' The immediate response of the candidate, 'Only to Christ'! This touching incident became widely known in the Mission/Church circles, as a very striking testimony (H.F.1938, p.23; Sargant, pp.11-12; MDR, 1922, p. 9).

The candidate in question was none other than R. Christadas, later to become a minister of the church.

CHAPTER – 6

Persecution, Drought, Starvation and Disease: A Saga of Pathos and Faith

There was an inexplicable feeling of solace among those who embraced the new faith. However, joining a new faith did not end their woes. In fact, their conversion into new faith increased their woes! Since they had embraced a new faith which was branded as alien or foreign, the neo converts had to face doubly more contempt. The public contempt against their conversion to a new faith was often turning into organized persecution, instigated mainly by the Hindu orthodoxy. Besides the recurring harassments andpersecutions which the neo converts had to face for the sake of their conversion to Christianity, the repeated spell of drought, diseases and pestilence also made the lives of poor neo converts literally unbearable. However, they stood astoundingly firm and it was truly a saga of pathos and faith.

Persecution- for Christ sake

The Hindu orthodoxy became increasingly agitated when a growing number of depressed class people began to embrace Christian faith in CN villages, right before its eyes. A fear was growing in Hindus that they might permanently lose Panchamas (MDR,1924, p.55)! So, they started making determined efforts to stop the conversions. They succeeded to a great extent in poisoning the minds of gullible Hindus against Christian Mission work and creating much antagonism. Fierce opposition became a common occurrence in almost every village where baptisms took place. Following were some of the major instances where violent opposition against conversions took place:

− **Kastur 1908:** there was fierce opposition when the first Baptisms in Kastur took place in September 1908. However, the community leaders and Sawday firmly dealt with the agitators. Madaiah (Christian name: Devadas), one of the first two converts of Kastur, played an important role in countering caste Hindu opposition against conversions in Kastur, firmly.

− **Bhogapura 1908:** In September 1908 two families were baptized in Bhogapur. They were the first converts in this village. In fact, more families were keen to join the Christian faith but due to fear of caste Hindus, many could not make a final decision. Their fear was based on the apprehension that they would lose their very livelihood if they convert to Christian faith.

− **Homma 1910:** In Homma, a village about eight kilometers from Kastur, eight adults and ten children took Baptism in 1910. A widow of this village, whose children were all slaves pleaded for baptism. During Sawday's subsequent visit to the village they were all baptized. Immediately there was a big commotion and backlash from caste Hindus in the village. It was reported, "In this new village our people have had more than their share of trouble. Social sanction was made on the newly baptized families-consequently no advance of grain which was customary. Wild rumors were spread against converts. People banded together to prevent us (missionaries) from getting foot hold in the village. However, our people stood firm." (MDR.1910 p.30)

- **Villages** (names not noted) **around Kastur 1911:** Due to growing violence against converts and the missionary work, missionaries had to slow down their work for a period. They concentrated more on consolidation of newly converted during that period. It was reported: 'early in the year (1911) some enquirers were severely beaten up by their masters, and this act of intimidation had its effect on the people, who naturally timid and easily frightened (MDR, 1911 p.41).

- **Kastur and Bhogapura 1912:** In 1912 Plague was taking heavy toll in CN villages including in Kastur and Bhogapura. Many among Christians died. It was reported that the 'heathen neighbors rejoiced and told that plague came because they (the converts) had given up worship of gods who are angry with them' (ref, MDR, 1912, p.34). However, the missionaries testified that there were hardly any cases of relapse among the converts of going back to their old faith.

- **CN villages 1914:** Devastating drought in CN villages. Along with all other villagers Christians too suffered untold misery. Firstly, they suffered due to a terrible drought; secondly none would give them coolie work because of their conversion to Christian faith (MDR, 1914, p.40). It was a social boycott on them. It was reported that many Christians of Mysore city helped those village Christian families in despair, at that time.

- **Name of village not noted-1915:** Three families were baptized. However, head of one respectable family was being kidnapped two miles away to prevent his baptism. In this situation a strong detachment of Christians went there and brought him back (MDR, 1915, p.25). Such display of unity and resistance was not too rare among Christians,in fact increasing.

– **Hadya 1922:** On 18th October 1922 twelve adults and ten children were baptized in Hadya. The day before the baptism a lot of fear was created among the enquirers and false propaganda widely circulated against the missionaries. Their malicious propaganda included, 'If you join Christian faith you will not get marriage alliance for your children. Your taxes will be increased. Your children will be seized and sent over the seas so that you will never see them again' (MDR,1923, p.53)

– **Kirugunda 1923:** This was the village where one of the more serious violence took place against Christian Mission work and the neo converts. The violence was instigated by Hindu orthodoxy led by Brahmins of the noted temple town Nanjanagudu as well as Mysore. It had become very difficult for the Hindu orthodoxy in Nanjanagud to watch many families embracing Christian faith in their neighboring villages, like Kirugunda and Hadya.

The incident that flared up commotion in Kirugunda was the baptism of fourteen adults and five children. The agitators stirred up people with wild and false rumors in Kirugunda and the surrounding villages. They set people against the missionaries. They behaved rudely and violently with the evangelist, those baptized and the enquirers who were about to be baptized. They had even enticed the enquirers that they would be given lands if they remained in their old faith. Further a particular vernacular news paper of pro-Hindu leanings, published from Mysore city, was circulated and provocative reports was spread saying that riots took place in Kirugunda on the day of the baptism and that Sawday used gun at the time and several people were injured!

There was some peace in the village for a period but after a few months the violence erupted again against the baptized and the enquirers in Kirugunda. However, by this time the little Christian flock had become quite assertive. It was reported that all caste Hindu harassments were firmly resisted by the newly converted families, with Christian families from surrounding villages also giving active support to them.

– **Kerehalli, 1923:** The same group which had instigated violence in Kirugunda created the trouble in Kerehalli village also. As noted, earlier instigators were all part of the Hindu orthodoxy. The occasion in Kerehalli was the baptism of seven adults and four children. Gurushanthappa was the leader of the group of the people who were keen to embrace Christian faith. He was summoned by the revenue officer and was badly humiliated and abused. He was twice struck on the face (MDR, 1923. p. 53). More about this courageous witness Gurushanthappa is noted in a later chapter.

– **CN villages, 1924:** Mounting false and vicious propaganda against Sawday and Wesleyan Mission by the news media based in Mysore City. A call was made to the general public that all Hindus should boycott all schools, dispensaries and all other institutions run by the Christian Mission (MDR, 1924, p. 56 ff).

– **Hadya, 1939:** Early in 1939, 55 people were baptized in Hadya, a village not too far from the temple town, Nanjanagud. This was the village where first conversions took place as early as in 1922. The commotion that was created by Hindu orthodoxy has been already explained in earlier section above. As the agitation mounted against the conversions as many as 35 out of 55 were forced to return to their old faith. One family, those of the community leader however returned to Christian fold again, after a while.

The converts together with the support of all Christians from surrounding villages resisted the further violence of Hindu orthodoxy, quite successfully (MDR, 1939, p.4).

Attempt to set fire to Hardwicke High School

In 1942, when the Quit India Movement had created politically a volatile situation there was an attempt set on fire Hadrwicke School, the famed educational institution of Wesleyan Mission, in Mysore city. However, the miscreants did not succeed (Sargant, p.62).

It must be noted that the above noted instances are just only few cases for reference and not inclusive of the countless instances of violence committed on missionaries, native ministers, newly baptized and the enquirers.

Few observations

Following observations throw more light on the pattern of persecution committed on them during the first 3-4 decades of 1900s in CN area:

Upper castes wanted the depressed class people to remain living in debased condition

The caste Hindu community, especially the upper caste section generally did never appreciate the depress class people coming out from their inhuman ordeal. They wanted them to remain in the same old debased and dehumanized condition. Conversion to Christian faith was obviously perceived as losing control over the depressed class people.

Upper caste people were always the prime beneficiaries of Mission institutions; but they only developed great contempt against Mission work

Although the upper caste sections were the majority beneficiaries of all Christian institutions, especially schools, ironically, they developed a great deal of contempt against missionaries and increasingly engaged in anti-missionary activities. For example, their agitation/dissent against Bible teaching in schools continued for years and it was a bone of contention, for long.

Brahmins and Lingayats gave the lead in anti-Christian agitation; but gullible lower castes too would meekly follow them

Generally, Brahmins along with other dominant caste people like Lingayats gave leadership to violent protest against missionaries/ new converts. In the process the rest of the caste Hindu people, most of them very gullible, would join hands, meekly.

Every time there was drought, disease and death struck in village, Christians were blamed

It was a common occurrence that whenever there were disease and pestilence Christians were held responsible. It was blamed that since Christians gave up worship of village gods and goddesses entire village was under the wrath of gods, therefore diseases and pestilence occurring (ref. MDR, 1912, p.34; MDR, 1943, p.10).

Ironically, few Gandians too joined hands with anti-missionary agitators

It is ironical that few freedom fighters or Gandhians also had joined hands in anti-Christian tirade/ agitation as well as in false propaganda against Christianity. An important example was the well known freedom fighter Thagadur Ramachandra Shastry who had persistently campaigned against missionaries in Mysore district to which CN villages then as a taluk belonged. Thagadur's village Thagadur was in fact located just 6kms from Hadya, where one of the violent anti- missionary protest had taken place. Besides Hadya village, Kirugunda and Kerehalli were other two villages which were worst affected by Thagadur's vociferus anti-missionary activities in those years.

Oppressive 'Disability' Law

A law of the land itself such as the 'Disability Act' served as an instrument of oppression and deprived freedom of religion, justice and dignity to the depressed class people and to those embraced Christian faith. Reference about this oppressive Act and how missionaries protested against it was already made in previous chapter.

Media active in spreading anti-missionary propaganda

Vernacular media based in Mysore had become one of the main instruments in malicious anti-Christian campaigns. The tirade of propaganda made against missionaries in 1934 was particularly reported in detail in Mission reports. A news paper 'Mysore Patriot' took a vicious campaign against all the missionary work, particularly on Sawday.

Anti-conversion bill placed; but failed to get mandate

In 1939 an anti-conversion bill was placed before the State Council. The proposed Bill was intended to bring entire conversion process under strict bureaucratic control. However, the Bill failed to become an Act due to the failure in getting required support in the Council (Sargant, p.51).

Enticement, spreading rumors, threat

Enticing/ inducing, frightening, falsely fixing the enquirers and so on were among the countless ways to demoralize neo converts/ enquirers. They were enticed through promises of monetary benefits to stay/return back to old religion. The enticing monetary benefits included, money, free housing sites, lands etc. While those inducements or 'bites' made an impact on people, the stories galore how the neo converts and enquirers ignored those monetary benefits. The malicious frightening of people included: if converted they will not get marriage alliance to their sons and daughters, their taxes will greatly increase, their children will be seized and sent over the seas, never to see them again. And of all it was usually the gullible women folk who were easy prey to the baseless propaganda (MDR, 1922, p.46). The Wesleyan Mission report of 1923 gives an account of how the agitators extensively tried monetary benefits to block baptisms in Kirugunda (MDR, 1923, p.53).

In fact, the inducement method was tried in all most all the CN villages to block conversions.

It goes to the credit of young congregations that generally Christians stood firm in their faith.

The inhumane social sanctions against Christians

Social sanction namely boycott of the newly baptized families was one common and inhumane punishment given to the newly converted. Social boycott barred all the newly converted from entering village, denied them coolie work, entry to provision stores and thus made their life utterly miserable. The social sanctions which were laid on the converts especially during the famine times were inexplicably inhumane (MDR, 1897, pp.9-10; MDR, 1910, pp.30-33; MDR, 1914, p. 40). It may be noted that those social sanctions were in addition to regular caste oppression meted on them.

Christians knew well before hand, what lies before them if they convert

It was revealing that most of the enquirers knew well ahead what lies before them if they become Christians (MDR, 1923, p.55). They knew well that if convert they will be losers only (MDR, 1897, pp.9-10). Persecution, harassment and so on were waiting for them, if converted. Despite that, those who made a final decision for Christ generally did not retract but stood firm.

Amazing faith that made new believers stood firm

It is revealing that in the face of countless trial and tribulations which the neo converts faced they generally stood remarkably firm. No amount of opposition, harassment, grinding poverty, enticements or even persecution tempted them to retract/ relapse. Their faith and patience were often deeply praised by the missionaries (MDR, 1912 p. xi; etc).

Ravaging diseases and droughts

Diseases and drought were typically a recurring event every alternative year in CN area. Cholera, plague and smallpox used to greatly devastate lives of people almost regularly. In addition, fatal influenza was also ravaging very often. When there was an outbreak of contaminating diseases like plague or cholera people, along with their little herds of livestock, used to shift to temporary sheds outside the village, for isolation. On such occasions schools would close down and it was a standstill and anxious-filled time.

Generally, when fatal diseases used to strike, they affected everyone in villages, rich or poor. However, the worst victims were always the poorest section of the population to which Christians belonged. In 1920 the missionaries reported that the full membership in CN village churches had reduced from 600 to 500 mainly due to the onslaught of above noted diseases, especially plague. Starvation, malnutrition, acute shortage of drinking water, recurring drought condition, poor housing condition, a general lack of sanitation/ health awareness were all contributing for the spread and recurrence of epidemics.

Further, people in some of the villages of CN area were suffering from the wide spread leprosy. Again poverty, scarcity of water and lack of sanitation were found to be primary reasons in the spread of this disease.

Strangely, whenever Christians were affected by cholera or plague, they had to face the ire of the villagers. Villagers would say "you gave up gods' worship therefore now you are punished" (MDR, 1912, p.34).

Devastating diseases striking, year after year

In 1912, referring to an ongoing ravaging drought, missionaries reported "that had been busy, sickness still rife, and the crops had failed" (ibid). It was added that people silently suffered and not murmured. The missionaries also noted that despite the untold misery which the newly converted had to face, by and large, there were no cases of relapse to the old faith.

It appears the year 1918 and 1919 were the most miserable time for the CN village Christians. The year 1918 was the World War I period. During that year people suffered the worst from diseases as well as drought. First it was smallpox then it was cholera, and then came drought and finally the dreaded influenza! It was endless. All those took heavy toll of people and property. Since parents succumbed to fatal diseases, children in many families were left as orphans.

As an effect of WW-II it was also a time of starvation and misery. It was reported: 'Often there was not even one meal a day. The grain had become dearer; people had no money to buy. There was no kerosene oil to light lamp. Many people died. People wandered from market after market but returned empty handed' (MDR, 1918. pp. 40-43).

Sawday reporting on the miserable condition wrote: "We have never known such terrible sickness as we had in 1918. Plague and cholera devastated the country side. .... causing misery such as cannot possibly described" (MDR, 1918, p.63). He also added how the prices had gone sky high, higher than even that of Great Famine time in 1877-78. He had reported how after the turn of plague and cholera, influenza had struck people in which thousands of people especially those who were weak and old died.

Widows everywhere

The following year i.e., 1919 too was a year of great misery. There were widows everywhere. Sawday wrote that when they went to villages in early 1919, they found widows everywhere! Many villages turned as a depressing sight with a large number of widows. Missionaries tried to help people as much as possible, but the need was so enormous and it was extremely difficult to cope with it (MDR, 1919, p.63).

However, in spite of the intolerable suffering which those people underwent especially during 1918-1919 they stood firm in their faith. Sawday wrote "in spite of their extreme need there has been no grumbling on the part of the people" (MDR, 1919, p.64). The missionaries and the native ministers on their part strengthened the neo converts through their preaching and teaching especially through reminding them of the great trail and tribulations many heroes of faith in Bible as well as in the early church had to undergo.

The year 1925 had again become a year of great misery. Besides plague, influenza inflicting people, a long period of dry spell added to their woes. Since there was no coolie work available in their village large number of people began migrating to coffee estates. However, many died on their way or after reaching the place. Many suffered due to various diseases including hookworm. Many lost their husbands and families lost their bread winners. It was reported in 1925 that there were as many as above 50 widows in the CN village congregations (ref. Sargant, pp.18-19 and MDR, 1925, p.55).

The Mission report of 1928 narrates how people greatly suffered around that time due to a very prolonged drought of 5 years. Wells were totally dried up. Women used to walk a long distance to fetch some water. Missionaries tried to deepen some wells but with little success (MDR, 1928, p.58). A striking incidence of human kindness was also reported. It was reported, though the name of the village not noted, how 'a Christ-like caste man gifted a piece of land in low-lying area, where Christians dug a well and got water' (Ibid).

No respite to diseases and droughts in CN area

It appears diseases and droughts had no respite in CN villages! During the 5 decades when Wesleyan Mission worked in CN area at no time it was free from devastating diseases like cholera, plague, influenza or natural calamities like recurring drought. Leprosy was yet another disease which pestered people in number of villages of CN area. For the missionaries working in the area with a very hapless people whom none took too seriously, it was often a stupendous task, a strenuous 'swimming against the stream' experience. However, they never gave up.

A saga of pathos and faith

'Death had been busy, sickness was still rife, and the crops had failed' (MDR,1912, p.34)

It was indeed a great saga of pathos and faith for village Christians. It was difficult for caste Hindus, particularly the Hindu orthodoxy to accept their conversions to Christian faith, which their poisoned minds continued to believe as a 'foreign' or 'alien' religion. On the other hand, they were continued to be dehumanized because of their 'untouchable' origin. Thus, they were victimized on both counts, first their SC origin and second their conversion to Christian faith.

However, their woes did not end there. Nature was not very kind to them. The recurring drought in the area was battering people and livestock. Adding to this there was chronic outbreak of contaminating and fatal diseases which used to take heavy toll. Droughts, pestilence or diseases did not have favour or prejudice on any one; they were impartial in their devastating effects, including the Christian community.

As early as in 1912, Sawday reported about the saga of pathos and faith of CN village Christians which they were passing through.

He stated, 'The simple villagers in that remote church have been called to encounter persecutions, privation, sickness and death, but in their experience, it has been proved once again that the promises of God are inherited by faith and patience.' (MDR, 1912, p. xi). It was striking that the people got themselves baptized although they knew very well that much trouble was ahead of them (MDR, 1923, p.55).

The missionaries and evangelists used to spend more time with the new believers when they were facing testing times like persecutions, drought or disease (MDR, 1911, pp.41-42). The evangelists used to console and strengthen them by telling them stories of heroes of faith in the Bible.

It was a time when 'the cup of tribulation was full to the brim'. Amidst this continued the saga of pathos and faith of the new believers.

CHAPTER – 7

Amazing Missionary Spirit of Village Christians

It is striking that the planting of churches in the villages of CN area is very distinctly a lay movement. True, a host of pioneer missionaries along with the native associates had labored hard in the area; however, it was significantly the village Christians who were the prime torch bearers of the Good News. It was the overwhelming missionary zeal of the new believers which enabled the Gospel to reach from village to village and from mouth to mouth. It became the singular concern of those simple folk that their kith and kin, living far and near, should also come to the feet of Jesus. It must be noted that the remarkable missionary zeal of people had been, time and again, acknowledged and profusely appreciated by the missionaries, working in the CN area during the first half of last century.

Missionary acknowledgment of the outreach spirit of village Christians

The missionaries saw that the spread of the Gospel and the planting of most churches in CN area were primarily due to the overwhelming zeal of the new believers. People were very eager that their kith and kin also embrace Christian faith. In 1912, when the CN village churches were still in their infancy the missionaries stated, 'The work is growing because of the converts, their devotion and enthusiasm. They have done all they can do to bring their non-Christian friends to the feet of Jesus' (MDR, 1912, p.50). In 1919 it was again reported, 'God is working through our people. Many of them have intense desire that none of their relations shall be left outside the fold of Christ and this is the spirit that will win the victory for the cross' (MDR, 1919, p. 66).

Sawday reporting in 1922 clearly affirmed: "the work in the Kastur neighborhood continues to grow deeper. As from the beginning, it is missionary spirit of the people which had spread the Kingdom. As soon as the man become Christian, he becomes anxious for the conversion of his friend" (MDR, 1922, p.8). Sawday adds how those new Christians share their Christian experience to others, mouth to mouth.

In the same year i.e., 1922 Sawday had reiterated his appreciation of village Christians' zeal to win over their unreached people. He stated 'my chief cause for gratitude is that all over people are so greatly in earnest in spreading the gospel of Christ and winning their relatives and friends for him. The work has thus far spread from village to village in this way' (MDR, 1922.p, 48). In fact, Sawday discloses that from the very beginning of its work in CN villages the Mission had aimed that their converts would be missionaries, who should take the glad tidings of salvation through Christ to all their non-Christian relations and friends. Sawday felt overwhelmingly gratified to see 'how eagerly the people, no matter how great their poverty, have striven to bring their friends to the faith of the Savior' (MDR, 1922, p. 45).

In 1924 Sawday again expressed his deep appreciation about the Missionary spirit of CN village Christians. While referring to few baptisms which took place in a CN village, Sawday stated, 'it is largely through their efforts that these men were baptized. In fact, nothing gave me so much joy than their determination to win people for Christ. There is in many of them a passion of desire to spread good news of Christ' (MDR,1924, p.55).

Missionary Hill based in Mysore, had acknowledged, 'the remarkable missionary spirit of the new believers was a pleasing characteristic of Kastur converts'. He added how those 'people were keen on getting their non-baptized relatives and caste men to become partakers with them of the blessing of the Gospel of Christ' (MDR, 1923, p.52).

Few outstanding lay men and women church planters to be remembered

While all the newly converted carried a great zeal to win over people to Christ, a few among them remarkably stand out since they made significant contribution in the planting of churches in CN area. Some of them were being called by the missionaries in those days as 'unofficial evangelists' and their service was well utilized in the planting and growth of new congregations. Their life and work are greatly inspiring and it should be remembered for posterity. A few important among them are noted here below though the information now available about them is very little. Further, it should not be surmised that the list here below is inclusive.

Isaac Kangani and his wife, CN town

It may be concluded on the basis of the records available that Isaac Kangani and his wife were the first ever Christian converts from CN area. He was living in Panchama keri of CN town. Sometime around 1870s along with his wife he went to Ceylon to work in the tea estate. There they came in contact with the CMS Tamil

Coolie Mission and were attracted to Christian faith and soon embraced Christian faith. The hard working and enterprising couple came up in life well and Isaac became an overseer (Kangani) in the tea estate. Since they always aspired to be with their kith and kin in CN town the Kangani family finally returned back to their native place in 1893.

Both Isaac Kangani and his wife had remarkable missionary zeal. They made their home in Panchama keri as a Christian worship center and also started a school there. For many years the small first Wesleyan Mission congregation of CN town/ area gathered there for worship. Kangani's home soon became a nucleus of devout Christian activities. Throughout their life time they labored tirelessly to win over their kith and kin for Christ. Further, through their devout Christian life and witness they set an example. However, the light which they had kindled in CN town did not grow as a movement, facilitating the growth the church. The congregation which Kangani's nurtured remained a tiny flock without any noticeable growth. However, the remarkable missionary zeal of Isaac Kangani and his wife, the first converts of CN are a great inspiration to be remembered always for the posterity. For more details refer to the earlier section in chapter III.

Muddayya (Abraham) and Madaiah (Devadas) brothers, Kastur

The story of these two brothers is very important in the history of churches in CN area. In fact, the conversion of these two brothers to Christian faith in 1908 is a milestone in the history of Christianity in the region. Their conversion triggered a remarkable 'Christ ward movement', beginning from Kastur and spreading into many villages. The details of the conversion of the two brothers had been already given earlier in chapter III.

The two brothers who were named after their baptism as Abraham and Devadas became strong pillars of the church not only in Kastur but in the entire region. Tireless seekers after truth, after a period of indecision, both had become fully devout in their Christian piety, filled with unsurpassing missionary zeal. As the Christ ward movement spread into villages, both Abraham and Devadas actively supported the work of the missionaries. Their indigenous caliber and remarkable acumen became a source of great strength and support to the pioneer missionary Sawday and others. Abraham was considered as a man of wisdom with great knowledge. People addressed him 'Upadru' (teacher). Besides agriculture he settled as a tailor in Kastur. Whereas his younger brother Devadas became an enterprising business man and actively supported the missionaries in planting of the churches. He was also a generous donor. He carried qualities of a good leader which greatly helped as more and more churches were planted. When the young congregations had to face severe persecution and harassment it was Devadas who stood strongly by with Sawday and effectively confronted the problems. The words of both the brothers Abraham and Devadas carried great weight within all the churches as well as outside, in CN area.

It may be stated that Abraham and Devadas brothers were the chosen vessels of God and truly the founding fathers of CN churches.

Swamydasa and Gurushanthappa, Mangala Hosur

The church in Mangala Hosur was the third one to be established in 1909, after Kastur and Bhogapura congregations in 1908.

It was Swamydasa, baptized in 1909, who made a remarkable service in the planting and growth of the church in Mangala Hosur. Swamydasa had an interesting background: for some time, he was a teacher in a village Mission school. He had an intelligent knowledge of Christianity. After working as teacher for some time he went to Ceylon and worked there as a supervisor (kangani) of coolies in a tea estate. Then he returned to his native place. Seeing his good knowledge of Christian faith, the Mission decided to employ him to help the evangelist in his village work (MDR, 1909, p.35).

Gurushanthappa was father-in-law of Swamydasa and the patriarch of Holeya community. Gurushanthappa, his wife and his three sons were subsequently baptized after the baptism of Swamydasa. It may be noted that both Swamydasa and Gurushanthappa became the strong pillars of the Christian community and contributed a great deal in the growth of the churches in Mangala Hosur and surrounding area (MDR, 1909 pp. 35-36 in Sawday's report).

Sundararaju, Hadya

Sundararaju was a native of Hadya who married to a girl in Mangala Hosur and was working there. While in M. Hosur, he embraced Christian faith. After some time, he returned to Hadya where his mother and younger brother were living. In Hadya he became a pioneer missionary. He brought a number of people to Christian faith and thus laid the foundation of a congregation in Hadya in 1922. At a time, Mission staff were less. Sawday greatly appreciating Sundararaju's commitment reported 'if all our people thus become living witnesses for Christ (like Sundararaju) the task will be accomplished and the world will be won for him' (MDR, 1922, p. 49; also, Sargant, p.11).

Chinnappa, Madapura

Chinnappa (man of gold) was a native of Madapura, then known as Madigahalli, which was located north of CN town on the main road. Chinnappa embraced Christian faith in 1921. Very much like his name the man had a very amiable and noble character. Though a new convert he carried an overwhelming zeal to reach others with the Gospel. Sawday reported how the night before the first baptisms in Hadya in 1922, Chinnappa came all the way from Madapura to Hadya, after making a difficult journey, and spoke two hours to the baptismal candidates telling his own joy of Christian experience till late in the night. Sawday rightly noted, "the people may not take in all that we tell them, but they are unable to gainsay what one of their own men saying, for every word can be touched." (MDR, 1922, pp.48-49) Chinnappa lived a devout and upright Christian life, full of missionary enthusiasm and ready to help anyone in need. He greatly contributed to the growth of the Christian faith in Madapura village and in surrounding villages of the area.

Gurushanthappa, Kerehalli

Kerehalli is a village located west of CN town. Gurushanthappa was a large land holder in the village and the chieftain of his community. In 1923 he embraced Christian faith along with few others in the village. Their conversions ignited a great deal of protest from the Hindu orthodoxy. A big commotion was created in the village. The trouble creators were the same people who created much problem to missionaries in Kirugunda and Hadya. They were all instigated by the Hindu orthodox elements based in temple town of Nanjanagudu and Mysore.

The newly converted community in Kerehalli was subjected to serious threat and harassment of various kinds. Gurushanthappa as the leader of the flock had to bear the brunt of all the persecution. He was assaulted and repeatedly harassed. The opponents also tried their best to induce the new believers to return back into old religion by offering them some benefits. But they did not succeed in those efforts. The Christian families stood firm and it was during that prolonged critical period, Gurushanthappa gave an outstanding and most courageous leadership holding the little flock together in all the adversities. He was a very faithful custodian of his people and his new-found faith until the last. It was said of Gurushanthappa: 'nothing will shake his faith (MDR.1938, p.7; also, MDR. 1923, p.53 and Sargant, p. 14).

A house wife and two brothers, Tiganare village, 1942

Tiganare was a village located to south east of CN town. The first baptism in this village had taken place in 1942. In August 1943 there were more conversions in Tiganare. The key persons who facilitated those conversions were a house wife, her husband and his brother. The brothers were from Madapura working in Tiganare. One of the brothers had married the woman who was a former Calvert boarding school student in Mysore. The Wesleyan Mission report of 1942 reports about the conversion as follows: "there are many connections with the Kastur villages, and it would be no exaggeration to say that this latest converts (in Tiganare) have come to Christ almost entirely through the influence and witness of two Christian brothers from our church in Madapuram, who have made their home in this village some years past. The wife of one these brothers is a girl from our Calvert Girls Home and it has been delightful to see her very real Christian influence in the village" (MDR, 1942, p.9).

The very active role which the village Christians played in the planting and the growth of the church in CN area is a unique feature of history of Christianity in this region. A report in 1939 states 'in the Kastur villages, the church is growing because of the witness given by the new Christians. When district evangelist were engaged in evangelistic work some of the elders in the village churches walked a long distance just to tell their friends and relatives what great things the Lord had done for them and their families. We are glad to find that the village Christians has taken witness bearing seriously" (NCCR, 1939, p.266).

Even as much later as in 1946 Hill reported: 'Six young men came from 40 miles bringing a young man for baptism' (MDR, 1946, p.8). This brief statement vividly points out to the remarkable missionary spirit the neo converts carried.

CHAPTER – 8

Empowering the New Community: An Indomitable Task

As the Christ-ward movement spread into many villages in CN area and an increasing number of congregations were founded, the missionaries were faced with the urgent but indomitable task of empowering the new community. Understandably, the large majority in the new community were continuing living in a dehumanized condition due to their Panchama social origin. The majority of them were living in abject poverty, illiteracy, ignorance and many as bonded labourers/slaves. How did the missionaries set themselves to the task of empowering those people who were spiritually and socio-economically at the lowest ebb is very revealing. The integrated way so with which the missionaries approached the problems and thus tried to empower an extremely vulnerable community is indeed greatly relevant even today.

Spiritual nurture of the young congregations

Wesleyan missionaries, very much like other Protestant Missions working in India at the time were of pietistic orientation. They upheld a good spiritual nurture of believers as supremely important, primary and foundational. Repentance, acceptance of Christ as the personal savior, growing in Christian faith as a new creation, personal holiness were all very much basic to their spiritual perceptions. Equally important was their emphasis to reach the unreached with the Good News of Christ. As the Charter book of faith, BIble should be at the very centre and preaching, teaching, worship and breaking of the bread were all perceived as of primary importance to grow in faith.

The missionaries realized soon that a people who were in shackles for ages required a very special support. Thompson makes a very vivid observation on this: 'When the Panchamas come to us their imaginations are polluted by unnumbered generations of mean and squalid living, their intellects are stunted and darkened by an age-long deprivation of all knowledge, their wills have never been directed towards or exercised in moral effort, and their consciences are wholly uninformed; they need the long suffering, vigilant, and most charitable care of men and women, who possess the mind of Christ' (Thompson....p.189).

a) Well organized and vigilant pastoral care

For a community which embraced Christian faith seeking liberation, dignity and solace a vigilant and systematic pastoral care was of utmost importance. It is striking that by 1930 almost all the village churches in CN area had residential evangelists. In 1908 when the first conversions took place in Kastur there were just two evangelists in the area, one in CN town and one in Kastur, while in 1930 there were as high as 16 evangelists working in village congregations of CN area. This reflects the utmost priority the missionaries had given to the spiritual nurture of the new believers. It did not matter to them whether the Christian flock was small or large, whether it was located in accessible place or not. The well organized, regular and systematic pastoral care greatly helped a steady growth of churches in the area.

b. The remarkable role played by Tomlinson

The remarkable role played by the veteran missionary Tomlinson and his team of District Evangelists in strengthening the Christian nurture in CN villages had been well acknowledged. Sargant and Ward paying tributes to Tomlinson had stated: Tomlinson was instrumental in Christian nurture of villagers. Through Scripture memorizing, Bible study, songs made impact on semi literate people which became foundation of their faith (W.E.Tomlinson, A Memoir and Some Papers, Sargant and Ward, 1952, pp.18ff). Tomlinson also started publishing 'Bodhaka Bodhini' journal, which was particularly a helpful guide to pastors and evangelists in their work.

While Sawday was fully occupied in the administration of Mysore and CN circuits, expansion/planting of new congregations, building churches, parsonages and wells and institutions, liberating slave children and so on and on, Tomlinson on his part as head of the District Evangelistic Band for several years took a special interest to strengthen village Christians in Christian nurture (MDR, 1911, pp.41-42). Regular worship, pastoral home visits, prayer meetings, Bible study classes, women's fellowship, youth fellowship and so on became a routine and greatly helped in the spiritual nurture of people and the growth of the church.

c) A visible change or 'Transformation' in the life of new Christians

Time and again missionaries have recognized and appreciated the change or transformation which was steadily taking place in the lives of the newly baptized. Missionaries were well aware that the newly converted 'have lived long years in a community where drunkenness is common…, where many forms of immorality are rife and the marriage tie is very loosely held, and where many kinds of open sin are totally disregarded' (MDR, 1919, p.65). A people once steeped deep in drinking, endless squabbles and immoralities were now steadily changing, after their conversion. The villagers themselves, many of them, in fact Christians constant persecutors, could not hide their surprise while noticing the good change which was taking place in the life of the newly converted (MDR, 1919, p.65; 1910, p.30; 1916, p.31). Sawday even reported how the villagers sometime used to call the newly converted people as 'the people of shining face' (MDR, 1910, p.32).

Sawday himself often recognized and rejoiced at the steady transformation which was taking place in the life of newly converted. He stated in 1916, "it is only 8 years, but there can be few places in the world where greater changes have taken place in the hearts and lives of people" (MDR, 1916, p.31).

d) A self –supported people with a culture of 'Christian Giving' ingrained in them

Educating the young congregations in Christian giving was considered as one of the important parts of spiritual nurture. Missionaries believed that as much as it was important to plant congregations it was also equally important to make them self supporting. They wanted to see the members self supporting and not dependent on Mission. Missionaries made every attempt to realize that.

Along with that they also tried to cultivate a culture of Christian Giving in the new congregations, right from the beginning. True, most of the believers were poorest among the poor, living in abject poverty; nevertheless the value of Christian giving was taught to them, through various ways, rather painstakingly. The result of those efforts was very rewarding. As early as in 1891 the missionaries noticed that the native Christians were good givers even in their poverty (MDR, 1891, p.5).

As a result of rigorous Christian teaching a culture of giving/ offering their 'mite' as thanks giving steadily took deeper roots in the churches. Sunday Offering, Thanks Offering, special offerings, offerings in kind (grain etc.,) offering to District Missionaries Fund, Mysore Missionary Fund etc. became well established practices of Christian giving in the new churches, within a few years. When the Wesleyan Mission on the occasion of centenary of its founding in 1913 started a Centenary Fund, the CN village Christians also contributed to that event, with great enthusiasm.

Sister Tomkinson introduced a practice of 'Sawday Cup' in the churches as a way to promote Christian giving. According to this each family makes a commitment to keep aside one cup of grain daily as its 'mite' in support of the ministry. The house wife usually takes care that the pledge is adhered to.

There were also cases of people making substantial contributions which helped the Mission work and in the growth of the community. To sight a few cases: Devadas one of the first converts of Kastur gave a piece of land to Mission wok; another person, an ex-jitha boy now in good position redeemed a jitha boy by paying the amount (MDR, 1938, p.23).

As early as in 1909, when the congregations in CN villages were still in infancy the missionaries felt greatly happy to see not only the spirit of Christian giving but also their support to missionary work. Missionaries saw that though people were poor they gave gladly (MDR, 1912, p.36). The missionaries reported, "The outstanding features of the work are, first that the Indian church has begun home mission work by raising funds and sending forth its own evangelist...Secondly, Panchama church evolving"(Harvest Field,1909, p.106).

It was acknowledged with great appreciation how even widows and poor gave. They gave themselves (MDR,1919, p.64). Sister Tomkinson who worked among the women in CN villages for several years exclaimed, "Their (women) sacrificial giving is amazing, though they are poor'(MDR,1940, p.15).

e) Literature/ publication work

Wesleyan missionaries extensively engaged in literature work when they were working in Mysore province. Right from the beginning they noticed that people have great craving for printed literature since the spirit of enquiry was fast spreading (MDR, 1921, p.31). Missionaries also noticed that people have great hunger for education, especially English education.

Missionaries first started printing of Bible in vernacular, Bible portions, prayer books, pamphlets etc. Wesleyan Mission had started a printing press for that purpose as early as in 1839 in Bangalore. The main purpose of printing and publication was evangelization and spiritual nurture of the new believers. The work quickly expanded, and the Mission Press also started printing school text books and so on. In 1873 the press was closed down, however, after a few years a press was started in Mysore city under the leadership of Henry Haigh. Named as Wesley Press, it made a big name in the country for its quality printing.

It was from here Haigh started publishing weekly paper 'Vrithantha Pathrike' in Kannada from 1887 which had, at its peak time, a wide circulation, as high as 5500 copies per week. It was the first weekly paper to be circulated in villages. During 1920s and 1930s Wesley Press, under Thomas Gould as manager, made a nationwide name for its high quality in printing. Orders were placed from all over the country (Sargant, p.37). However, the 'Vrithantha Pathrike' unable to withstand the competition, ceased to publish from 1941, despite Tomlinson's great efforts to save it.

Educational work

To win souls and empower the new community

Wesleyan missionaries embarked on educational work from the beginning, primarily as an instrument to win souls for Christ. They believed that literacy or education will drive away ignorance and superstition which were rampant among people and lead them towards Christian faith (MDR, 1921, p.25). Further they realized that although the Proclamation or preaching Christ .... alone was not enough....no one who had Christ's spirit can be content to live among the needy men, women and children and only preach (MDR.1921. p, 25).

Their perception was that

- Education would help as an instrument to win souls.

- Education is the way to respond to the needs of the people.

- Education to empower the new community, socio-economically.

With this understanding the missionaries embarked on educational work in Mysore province including in CN area.

Further Thompson states that two factors prompted the Mission to enter educational work boldly: Firstly, desire of people for education and secondly, a supportive and encouraging government (Thompson, p.141). An illustration to people's remarkable level of desire or motivation for their children's education was the instance when four thousand people signed an appeal in nine languages and submitted it to missionary Hardy to open an English School, in Mysore in as early as 1853(MDR,1853, p.15). Hardy took this petition to England where it created a great deal of sensation, with many coming forward with contributions.

The Wesleyan missionaries who entered CN region during the last quarter of 19th century were shocked to see massive illiteracy among people, besides grinding poverty. They saw that in a context of rampant illiteracy, superstition, various social evils and oppression were thriving abundantly. Along with preaching of the Gospel they plunged into educational work opening schools for the depressed class, backward class people and girls. As noted in an earlier section:

Their first school in CN town was for the ***depressed class*** people.

Second one was exclusively *for **girls***, in Ramasamudram.

Third school which they started was again for *the **depressed class*** in Nagavalli.

Fourth school was for ***backward class*** in weavers' colony in CN town.

The above facts clearly point out to the priority the missionaries always had in their educational endeavors.

While in 1923 there were six Mission schools in CN villages in 1940 there were seven and in 1942 there were all together nine schools. Thus, Wesleyan Mission made a pivotal contribution to the educational advancement of a region which was once steeped deep in illiteracy. It also remarkably contributed for the literacy/ education of the down downtrodden sections of the population like depressed classes, backward class and women. Thus, the Mission helped in the progress of land and people greatly and facilitated in the dawn of a new era.

Reports say that the educational work of the Wesleyan Mission progressed well making remarkable contribution to the advancement of people in Mysore province. The statistics 1926 says there were as large as 11,000 children studying in Wesleyan Mission schools in entire Mysore province.

From 1930s Mission schools in some places began closing down. This was because of the inability to cope up with the exorbitant establishment charges of running schools. Further it was time the government schools were being opened in many places. Adding to these the economic depression was also forcing the Mission to cut down expenses drastically (Thompson, The Call of India... p.141; Sargant, p.32).

Empowerment of Neo converts through education

It did not take much time for the missionaries to realize that preaching alone was not sufficient but the need to respond to the dire needs of people was very urgent for a people living in steep illiteracy, poverty, debt trap, jitha and caste oppression. The missionaries from the beginning were also very particular that the converts did not become dependents on them/Mission. As early as in 1870s they even encouraged the converts to join the police force (MDR, 1875, p.19).

Missionaries saw that there was a crying need for education to open peoples' eyes, create awareness and get them socio-economically empowered. Therefore, the missionaries not only started schools in CN villages but also sent literally scores of children to schools, boarding schools, orphanages and vocational training centre based in Mysore, Tumkur and Bangalore. Undoubtedly this became a great blessing to the newly converted families helping them to get socio-economically empowered. Further, the education of children of newly converted families in Mission schools in

CN villages or in boarding schools and orphanages in Mysore or Tumkur, groomed them in a new culture and orientation, which was different from the caste ruled traditional culture of the villages.

Missionaries sent scores of girls from CN villages to boarding homes and schools in Mysore city. Similarly, large number of boys, including those who were redeemed from slavery was sent to Mission schools in Mysore or to the orphanage in Tumkur. In 1936 it was reported that Tumkur orphanage/ vocational training Centre had 50 boys from CN area alone (Statement of Mysore District Policy, 1936, p.4). Referring to Calvert Memorial Girls Home it was stated in 1936 that 'the influence of that boarding school has been inestimable in the raring of Christian womanhood in villages' (Ibid; also MDR, 1936, p.4).

However, not all appreciated the boys settling in other places after the training instead of going back to villages where the need was more (Thompson, pp.4-5). It was argued that such migration would impoverish CN village congregations. It was argued that the present method of educating CN youth outside was not advisable (Statement of Mysore District policy, p.5).

The sober effect on the village boys in orphanage in Tumkur was also on the same lines. Needless to add that the education which the CN village children were privileged to receive in Mission institutions greatly empowered them socio-economically and helped them to come out from a totally bleak future to a new life of opportunity, freedom, human dignity and empowerment.

Around 1936 the Mission was seriously thinking of starting a boarding home and a vocational training centre, in very similar line one in Tumkur, at Heggewadi village in CN area (Sargant, p.41). The purpose of this included to reduce the burden on Tumkur centre. However, the proposed plan never realized. Had that plan realized it would have been a great boon to CN Christian community. Even land was purchased for a training centre and a boarding home. Tomlinson took special interest in the whole initiative. Lack of funds was reported to be the reason why the plan was not executed (MDR, 1938, p.29).

After planning for a boarding home in CN town proper for a long time, one was opened in mid 1950s i.e. after 20 years it was planned. However, this boarding home does not exist now since it was closed down in 2014.

Medical Work

Wesleyan Mission started working for community health in CN villages from 1920s. The Mission hospital in Mysore city namely Holdsworth Memorial Hospital, founded in 1906 was already making a big name as a major healing centre. It was drawing patients not only from the city but from far off places, including CN villages, and far beyond the borders of Mysore province.

It was the recurring instances of diseases like plague, cholera, smallpox, and influenza taking heavy toll and rampant problem of quack doctors in CN area which compelled the missionaries to embark on medical work on a priority and urgent basis. They saw how in a context of rampant illiteracy and superstition the quack 'doctors' had a hay day in the villages and how they were exploiting the gullible villagers. Proper health education and sanitation were the crying need of the rural communities.

The missionaries first had a plan to start a hospital in M. Hosur. However, since they could not secure a suitable site there in time it was decided to have the hospital in Kastur. Soon Sawday started raising funds for this major medical project. Finally, in July 1922 a compact hospital was built and dedicated in the presence of a large number of people, from many villages and from Mysore city.

The doctor who was appointed to be in-charge of the new hospital was Miraj- trained, Dr. P. Yesudas. He was son of Rev. H. Premaka, a veteran native minister. Premaka was Hanumayya before his Baptism and was a native of Veerara Keri (present Karunapura), one of the oldest Christian settlements in Mysore city.

P. Gurushantha, who became the first Bishop of Mysore Diocese later in 1947, was a brother of Yesudas.

As a medical evangelist based in Kastur, Yesudas served for an uninterrupted 40 years with un surpassing dedication (Sargant, p.11). He was popularly known as "Kastur Doctor" in all the CN villages. Sargant wrote about his remarkable service stating 'one looks in vain for the name of any other Indian doctors' (Sargant.p12).

The very first year Yesudas treated one thousand patients! He would do the work of an orderly/attendant, a pharmacist as well as of a medical doctor, almost single handedly, with utmost dedication. People came for treatment from all the villages, as far as 50 miles away, far beyond Mysore territory. The hospital flourished greatly, and the missionaries were happy that 'it was a great help to evangelistic work' (MDR.1922. p. 51).

In 1947 the hospital treated 10,000 patients in one single year (MDR, 1947, p.28)

Medical work and caste obstacle

Interestingly in the initial period of the hospital most of the patients were from depressed class and Christian community. This was because the caste Hindus shunned away from coming to the hospital for the fear of getting polluted. Even when they eventually started coming, for quite a long period the caste Hindus were hesitant to drink 'mixture' (liquid medicine) given in the hospital for the fear of ritual pollution (MDR 1923, p.56). However, that apprehension was totally disappeared, with the passing of time. The hospital became a remarkable centre for healing and service, where scores of people from all over and from all religions and castes eagerly came with great faith.

The missionaries were much gratified that the hospital grew year after year giving 'new life and hope to countless thousands of poor sufferers' (MDR,1928, p.59). The missionaries stated, 'When we 'wanted to have hospital in Mangala (Hosur) people did not want to give us site; now they beg us to leave Kastur and come to Mangala' (Ibid).

Leprosy work by the Mission- a path breaking initiative
Noticing the extensive cases of leprosy in parts of CN area the Mission sent Dr. Yesudas to Calcutta for training in leprosy treatment. From late 1930s Yesudas was very much involved in leprosy treatment, besides managing the ever growing Kastur hospital and its weekly clinics in CN town and M. Hosur. Yesudas used to always say, 'leprosy is so easy to prevent, so difficult to cure' (MDR, 1937, p.37). He actively began intensive preventive propaganda on leprosy in many CN villages where cases were rampant. Undoubtedly, it was the first organized anti-leprosy campaign to be pioneered in CN region.

Extension work of Kastur hospital in CN villages
In 1925 Kastur hospital opened weekly dispensaries in a few villages (name not noted). Missionaries reported that in 1927 a weekly dispensary was opened in CN town on the repeated appeal of people there for women and children' (MDR, 1927, p.57).

In 1937 when there was a cholera outbreak the Kastur hospital immediately embarked on an intensive anti-cholera inoculation campaign (MDR, 1937, P.37). It was reported that when cholera took heavy toll, it was claimed by Christians that there was not even a single death in the Christian community.

A hospital was opened in Hadya in 1933 for which Dr. V. Abraham was made in charge. In 1943 Abraham was sent to Chingelpet for training in leprosy work (MDR, 1943, p.15). After his return he intensively engaged in leprosy work in southern parts of CN taluk where leprosy was quite a serious problem. Abraham passed away in 1944 while serving in Tiganare, a very difficult terrain in south of CN area, bordering Tamil country. An exhausted Abraham broke down and succumbed to malaria (MDR, 1944, pp.10-11).

Meanwhile, Kastur hospital and its weekly dispensaries in villages continued to render remarkable service and it became a great blessing to CN villages.

Work among women

The missionaries realized that women were potentially a great resource in the spiritual nurture and in the growth of the church. This realization made them to focus their work among women so as to utilize them to empower the Christian community. They also knew that in a caste based and gender- unequal society women face endless problems which were turning life of many of them miserable.

Thus, on both counts the missionaries started addressing the needs of women, in the congregations firstly as victims of an unequal society and simultaneously as potential partners in nurturing of the congregations.

Perhaps the first initiative of missionaries in this regard was to utilize the service of wives of catechists and evangelists. Later Bible Women and lady missionaries were recruited and posted in the CN area, regularly. They worked among women and children and greatly contributed to the growth of churches in the region.

The missionary reports mention about one Sanjeevi a Bible Woman in Mysore city and its suburbs in 1870s whose very dedicated service was highly appreciated. She was the first Bible Woman in Mysore region (MDR, 1876, p.45; 1874, p.35; Findley & Holdsworth, pp.278-79)

Catalytic role of Mission boarding homes and schools in empowering women

References were already made on how imparting of education had greatly empowered women. In that task the role played by especially boarding homes and schools was pivotal. In 1936 referring to Calvert Memorial Girls' Home the missionaries reported, 'The influence of that boarding school has been inestimable in the rearing of the younger Christian womanhood in villages' (Statement of Mysore District Policy,1936, p 4).

Role of Bible women

When the first conversions in Kastur began to take place in 1908 a Bible Woman was immediately posted there by Sawday. Along with the local evangelist Jonathan, the Bible Woman facilitated the conversions by meticulously preparing women folk for baptism. Thus, women played a remarkable role in the Kastur movement, right from the beginning. From mid 1920s onward, the work among women in CN villages began to take more organized form. Sister Ethel Tomkinson was appointed in 1925 as in charge of a women's work centre (Premalaya) in Kastur. There after the work among women and children was more intensified and organized.

More Bible women were appointed for the purpose. The Bible women gave a valuable support to the catechists and evangelists/ministers. Among the Bible Women who served in CN villages during the second quarter of the 20th century, include, Milcamma, Salomamma, Huldamma, Santhoshamma, Susanamma and of course as noted earlier, Sister Tomkinson who villagers affectionately called 'Premamma'. In 1943 there were as many as four Bible Women in CN circuit.

In 1923 the Wesleyan Mission started a Bible School for women at UK Seminary in Tumkur (Sargant, p.13). Olive Hornby was in charge of this school. There were 11 students when it started. This school became quite helpful in providing Bible women for the Mission work in entire province, including CN villages.

The main task of the Bible Women, including wives of evangelists in the villages included:

- *Spiritual nurture* of the congregation, especially of women and children.

- *Basic health education* to women by way of imparting awareness in health /sanitation

- *Social education* which attempted to clear superstitions, discourage caste practices

Role of wives of catechists and evangelists

As the number of village congregations increased the role of the wives of residential evangelists in Christian nurture became important. They visited homes regularly, did counseling, created health and sanitation awareness among women and children. Sister Tomkinson used to give orientation to the wives in Christian nurture, Christian Giving, health awareness and so on which was passed on to the community, via catechist's wives to women. Thus, the evangelists wives gave very vital support in the growth of the churches and played a valuable supporting role to their evangelist husbands.

Premalaya (Home of Love)

As noted earlier in 1925 Sawday established an ashram in Kastur, an institutional centre for women's work. This was a land mark event. Sister Ethel Tomkinson who was working in Mysore circuit was transferred to CN circuit and made in-charge of Premalaya. The centre included a prayer room, a baby clinic, a women recreation room and a modest house for the Sister-in-charge (MDR, 1925, p.59). The Ashram had a tailoring training section and also had a nursery for infants.

Subsequently the Mission opened an ashram for women, in Hadya also which came to be known as 'Chikka Premalaya' (little abode of love).

Tomkinson did a remarkable service in CN villages for a number of years. She used to travel with her medicine kit to villages in bullock cart and visit families. They were long and strenuous tours 'through dangers of swollen streams, tigers, elephants and wild pig...' (MDR, 1947, p.19). Along with spiritual nurture she used to create health awareness among women and children. She also mentored wives of catechists/evangelists providing them useful tips especially as related to family life, upbringing of children and health. The objective was to percolate those ideas among women folk in the congregations.

Temperance Movement - a campaign against alcoholism

Missionaries discovered that drinking toddy and alcoholic drinks was quite rampant among men folk in the congregations. They saw the devastating effects of drinking on people and their families, who were mostly living in abject poverty. This hastened missionaries to do something urgently against the growing drinking habit found among people in young congregations. The missionaries' reports indicate that they made organized efforts with this regard from 1920s onwards first in Kastur and soon in other CN villages to get rid of the evil of alcohol addiction. Their efforts were called temperance and it had met with quite some success.

Missionaries started organizing meetings for men, beginning in Kastur, to create awareness in them on the harmful effects of drinking on them, their families and community. Those efforts began yielding some good result. Soon, people volunteered themselves to make a pledge in the public to totally give up drinking. The Mission was happy to report that the leaders of young church were increasingly becoming strong advocates of temperance (William Goudie, General Secretary, WMMS, 1936, p.66). In one meeting a total of 70 young men's thumb impressed the pledge and submitted them against drinking. According to the rules they voluntarily imposed on themselves that if one breaks the pledge he had to pay a penalty of 5 pounds which was roughly 15 days coolie (Goudie, Secretary, WMMS, V, 1920-21, p.66; MDR, 1920, p.8). Sargant reported that in 1943 at the Circuit convention 100 youth pledged to give up alcohol (Sargant, p.60).

Opening tea shops- to divert people from toddy shop

During World War-II (1914-1918) when there was a good demand for silk, the silk industry flourished in CN villages (Sargant, p.60). Many families quite thrived in mulberry cultivation, rearing silk and yarn making. However, silk industry increasingly proved health hazardous to people. Worst thing to happen was as people's pockets filled with more money the habit of alcohol drinking started alarmingly escalating. Number of school dropout cases increased. Church attendance noticeably dropped. Observing all those detrimental effects, missionaries intensified temperance movement/ anti-alcohol campaign in the area. Mission opened tea shops to divert men folk hanging around toddy or liquor shops. The first of tea shop was opened in Kastur in1941. Sister Tomkinson, then in charge of Premalaya took an active part in the anti-alcohol campaign in CN villages.

CHAPTER – 9

Legendary Wesleyan Methodist Missionary George William Sawday (1854-1944)

A glimpse into his work in Mysore province, especially in Mysore and Chamarajanagara

Sawday- a great legendary missionary

George William Sawday was not just a missionary but a legend. Volumes could be written on the astounding work he had done in Mysore province, especially in Tumkur, Mysore, Mandya and Chamarajanagara area. Sawday lived for long, about 90 years and most of it, well over six decades he lived and served in Mysore province, a country which was so beloved to him. He breathed his last in Mysore, a city which was his home for 44 years.

A humble attempt of this writer

These few pages by this writer are a tribute to the legendary missionary Sawday. This writing is a humble attempt to catch Sawday's amazing life and work. Indeed, it is an indomitable task. Sawday is remembered even now by many especially by the older generations in Tumkur, Mysore, Mandya and Chamarajanagara, with great nostalgia. However just nostalgia will not suffice. The great liberative and the pioneer work done by Sawday in planting host of churches, liberating scores of people from the chains of slavery and founding/constructing land mark institutions should be remembered for posterity. His life and work should continue to be read and reread, reflected and researched afresh so that it can inspire the present and future generations of the community. This could greatly help in the revitalization and renewal of the churches which is indeed the crying need of the day.

Shortly awaited – The bicentenary (1821-2021) of arrival of Wesleyan Missionaries to Mysore province

It should be remembered that the year 2021 is the bicentenary year (1821-2021) of the arrival of Wesleyan missionaries to Mysore province. This historic event is not too far away. This writer will be more than happy if his writing may serve as a *preparation* for that great Bi-centenary event of thanksgiving and celebration in 2021. The need to perpetuate the work of the pioneer Wesleyan missionaries who served in the Mysore province, including the legendary missionary George William Sawday is very important and urgent in the context of the crying need for an urgent renewal of our churches today.

Early days of George William Sawday

George William Sawday was born in Sidmoth, Devon of England on 10th March 1854. His father was George Sawday and mother was Mary Ann Burt. After his primary and high school education in Surrey, he went to Lambeth (London) at the age of 16 for study. In 1873 he was accepted for Wesleyan Methodist ministry and began his ministerial training at Headingly College. At the end of the training he was ordained as pastor of the Methodist Church.

Sawday's family

On 28th November 1877 Sawday married Sarah Trot Curnock (1852-1895) in English Chapel (now, St Mark's Cathedral) in Bangalore. The couple got seven children, four daughters and three sons. Last two daughters died when they were infants, in 1891 and 1893. His children were born in India and lived in England.

Sawday's wife Sarah died in England in 1895 when the family had gone there on furlough. She was 42 years when she passed away. She was a very active woman who laboured hard along with her husband in Mission station at Tumkur. The series of deaths in the family, first two daughters and then his wife, must have dealt a terrible blow to Sawday. However, he continued to serve undeterred.

After his wife's death Sawday worked in England for some time, as a Methodist pastor. However, India was calling him, and he returned to Mysore province again in 1900 as missionary. He was 46 years old then.

Kunigal, Sawday's first station

As noted earlier, the young missionary Sawday arrived in India on November 24, 1876. He was 22 years then. The year 1876 is important because including Sawday three Wesleyan missionaries who rendered remarkable service in Mysore province entered India the very same year. The trio were J.A. Vanes who came early that year, Sawday and David Arthur Rees who came together in November. Rees was Sawday's life- long close friend. Rees, returned to England in 1926 after 50 years of service.

Sawday's first station was Kunigal, which was then called as Coonghul. The Mission station in Kunigal was one of the first stations started by the pioneer missionary Rev. Thomas Hodson, way back in 1838. During his Kunigal days Sawday's native associate was Samuel Solomon. Wesleyan Mission report of 1876 stated, 'Mr. Sawday has been appointed to Coonghul. This is one of the oldest stations, and he will find the field already partially prepared for the good seed of kingdom' (MDR, 1876, p.6).

Sawday's tenure in Kunigal was short since within a year he was transferred to Tumkur. The reports on Sawday's Kunigal tenure highlight following few things:

1) Sawday and evangelist Solomon used to extensively tour Kunigal and surrounding villages on evangelistic work.

2) He used to regularly conduct Sunday services in Kunigal in which about 20 very high caste and educated Hindus were also attending (MDR, 1876, p.11).

3) He baptized two adults and a child during his short stint in Kunigal.

4) A person who was interested in Christian faith ate together with the missionaries (Sawday). That created a big commotion in the town alleging that the man ate with a 'pirangi' or a casteless man and got himself ritually polluted. However, the man stood firm in his faith. With much courage he openly denounced and discarded caste and idolatry in his native village. On the following Sunday he took baptism in Kunigal town.

5) Sawday opened a school. The reports say that there was already a Mission school at Bidaranakere village, in Kunigal surrounding.

Sawday posted to Tumkur

Sawday was transferred to Tumkur in 1877. Shortly before that he was based in Gubbi for a short period. Sawday's arrival to

Tumkur heralded beginning of one of the most fruitful periods of his service which lasted up to 1895 uninterrupted, except for a period of furlough in England.

Great famine (1877-1878) - massive devastation

The Great Famine in the years 1877-1878 will be long remembered in history as the time of one of the most devastating famines in Mysore province and South India. The Wesleyan Mission report of 1877 stated: "The year 1877 will long be remembered as the year of famine in Mysore and southern India. In consequence of the long and unprecedented drought the crops utterly failed, the cattle having no pasture perished by thousands (and in spite of all efforts of governments and private), and tens of thousands human beings, also perished from hunger and various forms of diseases" (MDR, 1877, p.3).

John C.W. Gostick reporting in 1897 stated that about 1,250,000 people died in famine. Findley and Holdsworth noted that the famine swept away one-fourth of The Kanarese people (Findley and Holdsworth...p.282). Further Gostick stated that 'the women bore the stress of the famine with more fortitude than men' (Memorials of the Indian Famine of 1977, March 1897, p.95).

It was at this time of untold human misery the Wesleyan Mission plunged into action to give relief to suffering mass, as much as possible. Firstly, it opened three relief camps to temporarily shelter and feed the destitute children. Those camps were in Mysore, Hassan and Kadur. At the same time the Mission opened an orphanage in Tumkur for boys. Gostick labored to build the orphanage and in this task, he was assisted by young missionary Sawday. Mission also started an orphanage in Hassan for girls. While the responsibility of girl's orphanage in Hassan was on missionary RiddItt and on the native evangelist Henry Premaka, the responsibility of boy's orphanage in Tumkur was soon fully entrusted to Sawday.

Canarese orphanage

When the orphanage in Tumkur opened in 1877 it was known as 'Canarese Orphanage' (now CSI Vocational Centre) and was meant to shelter 200 destitute boys of famine from various relief camps in Mysore province. However, the devastation was so huge that the orphanage had to admit as many as 322 boys within a year (MDR, 1878, p.69) Not all the boys who were admitted survived. Ninety-five boys passed away within a few weeks or months due to diarrhea, dropsy and famine fever. Forty-two boys deserted the orphanage. Ten boys were claimed back by parents/ guardians. Finally, 175 orphans remained out of which 161 are in health (MDR, 1878, p.70).

Sawday worked tirelessly to build up the orphanage which gave a new lease of life to scores of destitute boys. On the one side he had to work on erection of ever more space to accommodate unforeseen rush to the orphanage. Along with that a hospital was built close by, to take care of the ailing boys. Same way a school was also built. The boys not only studied in the school but also were trained in farming, carpentry, mat making and so on. Some boys groomed to become evangelists.

In 1879 Sawday was being made in-charge of entire Mission work in Tumkur circuit, including Gubbi and Kunigal. Amidst all the heavily demanding work Sawday entered family life marrying Sarah Trot Curnock. After the marriage both toiled together in building up the orphanage as well as taking care of the entire Mission work in Tumkur area.

Christian settlements in Bethelur and Devanur

In the initial period government used to financially support the orphanage in Tumkur. But when the government support came to an end, Sawday had to struggle to raise funds to maintain the growing institution as well as its expansion. It was a great struggle to meet the expenses of an ever-expanding orphanage. It was at this time Sawday purchased large stretches of land and established two Christian villages named as Bethelur and Devanur. A third village named as Sawdaypura was acquired later. He also purchased acres of agriculture land in Muthsandra for self support of the orphanage.

Sawday used to arrange the marriages of orphanage boys who have come up of age with the orphanage girls from Hassan. After the marriage the young couple were given a piece of land in Bethelur or in Devanur and sent there along with a trunk, little cash, an oxen cart and some agriculture implements. Thus, he saw to a sustained development of boys who came once as totally destitutes. As the Christian settlements developed in both Bethelur and Devanur village Sawday built chapels there in 1886.

Few boys who had studied in normal school and did well in the study later took up jobs in the government or in private sector. Quite a number of young men from orphanage became catechists and entered fulltime ministry. Those who were trained in trades such as carpentry went to cities as far as to Poona and Bombay and many other industrial centres. True, there was a strong feeling among missionaries that the Chamarajanagara boys who were 'saved' and educated in Tumkur orphanage better return to their native villages and help supporting the Christian community there instead of migrating and settling down in other places (Statement on Mysore District Policy, 1936, pp.4-5).

In the midst of the laborious work Sawday had to face innumerable challenges, even from within. The task of sheltering the famine orphan boys, educating / training them in some trade which will guarantee them a livelihood and helping them settle in family life was taxing. Murmurings and quarrels within the community was not too infrequent. Sawday wrote in 1882, "Our hearts have often been pained at the tendency of our people to quarrel and their readiness to make offence at little things" (MDR, 1882, p.7). Later when Sawday was working in Mysore and Chamarajanagara circuits he had to encounter and deal with many such conflict situations in the congregations. Particular mention was made about an prolonged in fight in Kastur Church and how finally the two factions reconciled, sometime around mid 1920s (MDR, 1925, p.55).

Sara, Sawday's wife, was a great help during latter's tenure in Tumkur. She was helping mothers' meetings, helping in the supervision of Bible Women and assisting in running the schools and the orphanage.

After about ten years of continued service Sawday left to England on furlough in England in 1886. The annual report of 1886 is full of praise for his outstanding work in Tumkur on the eve of his departure to England. It was stated:

> He has been ten years on the ground, nine of them in Tumkur; and into those years he has put an amount and variety of service which all who know it envy, but not all can emulate. He has worked breathlessly all through, but neither hurriedly nor impatiently. Results surround him. The membership of his church has more than doubled; that chapel has been greatly enlarged and even so is often filled with worshipers; and the native pastor is now almost supported by his flock. The Orphanage, with more than 130 boys, has been a constant drain on his strength, wisdom and ingenuity, and constant test to his faith. He had been farmer, builder, and

mechanic, rope-maker and school master by turns, and older brother always to his boys, by watching opportunity carefully he has been enabled to establish two villages, surrounded by land which is now tilled by young Christian farmers. In all his labour he has found perpetual stimulus and most efficient assistance in Mrs.Sawday (MDR, 1886, p, 3).

Sawday returns to Tumkur after furlough – 1888

Sawday returned to Tumkur in 1888 after his furlough in England for little over a year. He continued consolidating the various work related to Mission and church in Tumkur area including the orphanage, school and Christian villages, congregations and so on. Andrew Philip was the native minister working along with him at that time and Christian Philip and Samuel Lamech were the evangelists.

Rev. Samuel Lamech- 'Mantri', wise counselor and friend of Sawday

From around this time Samuel Lamech (born in 1865), who hailed from Tumkur, became closely associated with Sawday. Lamech born of godly parents was a teacher in the Orphanage and store-keeper in the Industrial School. He joined ministry in 1901 and became a trusted associate, friend, 'manthri' or wise counselor of Sawday and leader of Indian ministers. (Sargant, p.6 and 33). Their bond continued lifelong. Lamech was later transferred from Tumkur to Mysore region where he worked many years with Sawday, shoulder to shoulder. Sawday used to affectionately address Samuel Lamech as 'Samuelayya'. Once after a difficult and marathon deliberation session with village Christians in Kastur Sawday wrote, 'Samuelayya rendered me the utmost assistance, indeed without him I do not know what I should have done'(MDR,1914, p.41). Some time in 1910s Sawday reported about a cart journey he made along with Samuelayya from Nanjanagud to Kastur. Sawday reported that the distance of 22 miles took 10 hours. Lamech retired in 1931 and died in 1947.

During his second tenure in Tumkur, Sawday worked for about six years, from 1888 to 1894. If his first posting is also included, he had served altogether a total of 15 years in Tumkur area. He played a pioneer and remarkable role in building a strong Mission base and a Christian community in Tumkur. Above all the Canarese Orphanage now named as CSI Vocational Centre, which Sawday established to shelter scores of destitute boys of Great Famine remains as an immortal and shining monument for his astounding labour.

Series of tragic events in Sawday's life (1891 to 1894)

As much as the work in Tumkur filled Sawday's heart with a great sense of fulfillment there was also sad events in a row, almost at the end of his Tumkur days. In 1891 he lost a daughter and again in 1893 he lost yet another daughter. Both died when they were infants. They were buried in Tumkur. The bereavement dealt a hard blow on the couple. Sawday and his wife by 1894 began to suffer serious health problems. Sawday returned to England with family in 1894. The same year Sarah, Sawday's wife, his inspiration and trusted partner, passed away. She was just 42 years when she died. Understandably the series of deaths in the family, firstly, two daughters and then his beloved wife, had greatly shaken Sawday. However, Sawday, after taking a break, started working as a pastor in England, first in South London and afterwards in Essex.

India calling

However, his desire to go back to India and serve the people there was very much alive deep in his heart. During the few years of stay in England, after his wife's death he established contacts and developed a large circle of friends and well wishers. Those contacts became a great boon in his later ministry when eventually he returned to India and started planting churches and establishing institutions. With India call ringing in his ears, Sawday returned to India in 1900, after six years of stay in England. India was going to be his home for the rest of his life.

Sawday posted to Mysore – A Golden Age of Wesleyan Mission begins

Sawday was posted to Mysore in 1900. Mysore was going to be his home for the next 44 years, till he breathed his last.

Mission station in Mysore was one of the first stations in Mysore province started by Thomas Hodson way back in 1838. When Sawday arrived in Mysore in 1900 his associates were E.W.Thompson, W.E. Tomlinson, both missionaries, T. Luke, Indian minister, and two evangelists, Masilamani and Whittaker. Rev. T. Luke was one of the first Kanarese ministers in Mysore province who passed away in 1920.

The Mission work was active in Mysore city and surrounding areas mainly through evangelistic campaigns in city, towns and villages. Open air preaching and sale/distribution of Scripture portions were main part of those campaigns. The educational activities of Wesleyan Mission work were also quite well known to the general public. A weekly news journal called 'Vruthantha Pathrike' which was started by missionary Henry Haigh in 1887 had quite a wide circulation. In its peak time as high as 5,500 copies used to be printed (Sargant, pp.6-7).

In Mysore city itself the Mission was running over half a dozen schools especially for the depressed class, backward class people and for girls. Those schools were slowly creating a social ferment among the downtrodden sections of the population. The Hardwicke English school/college was especially well known far and wide in the province. It was striking that in those days many of the bureaucrats, political leaders and eminent literary persons were all former students of Hardwicke institution.

However, the Wesleyan missionaries were carrying within themselves a grouse that their decades of labour had not yielded expected result. They always felt that the mass movement that took place in some of the neighboring states had never been the phenomenon in the Mysore province, despite long years of work.

Political transition

When Sawday was posted to Mysore in 1900, he was returning to India after nearly seven years of break. It was a period when Mysore province was enjoying relatively good political stability and progress. The province was under the administration of Mysore Maharaja under the supreme authority of British crown. The king Nalvadi Krishnaraja Wodeyar was very progressive and benevolent and the people held him in high regard. The royal family also always carried a high esteem on Christian Mission work. There were many instances when the Mysore kings gifted large chunks of land and financially patronized institutions run by Christian missionaries.

Mysore king Nalvadi Krishnaraja Wodeyar had a personal admiration for Sawday and regarded him as a wise counselor. Sawday had a special place of respect in Mysore palace/royal family circle. Reciprocally, Sawday and the Wesleyan missionaries held Mysore kings and the royal family with high esteem. They found the king was progressive, benevolent and impartial.

From the beginning of early 20th century nationalism was fast spreading. It was ironical that many of the nationalists especially in Mysore region equated Christian Missions with British imperialism and colonialism. Christian missionaries were held as pro-British and anti-national. Therefore, they tend to carry contempt against all Christian Mission work and Christian institutions. Their contempt was repeatedly expressed in various ways on many occasions in Mysore region. The unfortunate fact was that their misgiving on missionaries invariably joined hands with Hindu orthodoxy which always carried a chronic contempt against all non-Hindu religions, including Christianity. The total outcome was a growing hostility against all Christian work.

This was the situation or scenario when Sawday was posted to Mysore as head of the Mysore circuit as well as Chamarajanagara circuit.

A Golden Age of Wesleyan Mission begins under Sawday's stewardship

Mysore region provided a fertile ground to Sawday's inborn genius of planting churches and building institutions. With remarkable commitment and amazing zeal and energy he built institutions of long-standing significance in and around Mysore, one after another.

Sawday - The Master Builder

The following is a list of the main institutions/ churches he built or developed in Mysore city which is self explanatory:

1. **Girls Boarding Home** – 1901: The establishment of this boarding home gave a great opportunity for literacy/education of girls especially coming from the CN rural downtrodden section.

2. **Victoria Girls School** – 1903: Queen Victoria had supported establishment of this school. One of the famed schools of Mysore of the time. The school had made a big name at the all India level during the first half of the 20th century.

3. **Mary Calvert Holdsworth Memorial Hospital – 1905**: This hospital was built after Mysore was hit by plague in 1890,when thousands died. The founding of this Mission Hospital became a land mark event in Mysore city. The hospital became a great healing centre for entire Mysore region. Mary Calvert, married to missionary Holdsworth) was sister of Sawday, who had financially supported the construction of this magnificent hospital. Mysore Raja had taken a very personal interest in the founding and construction of this hospital. He donated the land for the hospital and also financially supported the work.

4. **Mary Calvert Girls Home – 1905**: This was yet another institution patronized by Mary Calvert, Sawday's sister and financially supported by her. This boarding home provided opportunity of education for hundreds of girls from Chamarajanagara villages.

5. **Enlargement of Wesley Church – 1906**: Wesley Church was the main place of worship for Kannada Christians in Mysore city for a long time. However, Sawday saw that the Christian community was growing and the building needed to be enlarged. Therefore, he enlarged the church by constructing the wings to it in 1906. This church is now named as Wesley Cathedral of Karnataka Southern Diocese.

6. **A Bungalow at V.V. Road, Mysore – 1908**. Sawday built on his own; it is now named as 'Sawday House' and recognized as a heritage building of Mysore city.

7. Construction of Guild Hall – 1911

8. Ladies Bungalow at V.V. Road – 1912

9. Girls School in Mysore and also in Hunsur 1930

10. Construction of Edga Church (Now named as Sawday Memorial Church)- 1931

11. Construction of Out Patient Block at Holdsworth Memorial Hospital – 1931.

12. Construction of Maternity Ward in Holdsworth Hospital -1938

It may be noted that the above list includes institutions and churches built by Sawday only in Mysore city. The list does not include the innumerable constructions by Sawday in other places like Tumkur, Chamarajanagara villages, Mandya and so on.

Sawday – The master church planter in Chamarajanagara area

Sawday will be remembered always as a pioneer hurch planter in Mysore province, especially in Chamarajanagara area.

a. Sawday and the spread of Christian faith in CN villages

It may be recollected that the Wesleyan missionaries then based in Mysore city used to visit few surrounding places of CN from early second half of 19th century. As far as CN town was concerned it appears that they could visit it only from 1870s. The relative remoteness or inaccessibility of villages must be the reason why they took such a long time to visit CN area and to open a Mission station there. However finally in 1885 they opened a Mission station in CN town and placed an evangelist there. But for reasons not known the years of missionary labour in CN villages did not yield much result.

As superintendent of Mysore circuit Sawday was also in-charge of CN circuit. He must have visited CN villages few times either on inspection or on evangelistic work, beginning from early 1900s. In the meanwhile, the CN villages remained a 'barren' land, for many more years.

b. The turning point- 1908

After years of 'drought' there was beginning of an unexpected harvest from the year 1908. In fact, the year 1908 could be rightly marked as the birth year of churches in Chamarajanagara area.

It all began with the conversion of two young brothers Mudda and Mada (after baptism named as Abraham and Devadas) who belonged to a Panchama family of good standing in Kastur. They were attracted to Christian faith while working in Waynad estates. When the parents heard about this they were agitated and forced the brothers to return back to their village. However, the two brothers were tireless seekers of truth and they continued with their search and struggle. At last they reached to a final decision to join Christian fold since they were convinced that the true peace and salvation could be found only in Christ.

The stories about these brothers and their spiritual struggle were reaching Sawday who was based in Mysore. Without further delay Sawday posted an evangelist one Jonathan to Kastur. He also appointed a Bible Woman to be based in Kastur. Both the evangelist and the Bible Woman prepared the brothers and their families for baptism and a group of thirteen people finally took baptism at the hands of Sawday on 14-9-1908. That was the birth/ founding day of the Kastur church. In fact, it was the founding

day of 'Kastur movement' with the Gospel spreading from village
to village in Chamarajanagara area.

From the historic year of 1908 till Sawday's retirement in
1932 over 13 village congregations were established, one after
another. In addition to this Christian presence was found in
several more villages. The congregations established from 1908
to 1932, until Sawday's retirement, included: Kastur, Bhogapur,
M. Hosur, Homma, Madigahalli (Madapura), Masgapura, Hadya,
Kirgunda, Kerehalli, Ugani, Basavahatti, Heggewadi , Kellamballi
and several out stations. Today most of the churches in CN area
are named after Sawday, a rare honour bestowed on a servant of
God who had for decades toiled in the region.

The establishment of above noted village congregations in
C N area came as an unforeseen bounty or harvest after a long
spell of drought. Missionaries' joy knew no bound! The news
about the conversions in CN area spread all over, far beyond
Mysore province, and reached global level also creating ripples
in Mission circles.

Through many catechists, evangelists, Bible Women and,
above all, missionary spirited village Christians were responsible
for that rich harvest together with the missionaries. However it
was none but Sawday who was both the master facilitator and
master planter behind the unforeseen harvest reaped in CN villages.

c.   Countless constructions–churches, parsonages, schools, hospitals, ashrams, housing for poor, wells etc.

With the Kastur movement in progress Sawday had no respite
at all. He purchased lands for the construction of churches and
parsonages. Sawday also purchased lands for housing the poor.
Since water was a serious scarcity in most of the villages, he

arranged to dig sink wells in more than 15 villages. Finding the rampant illiteracy everywhere Sawday opened many schools. Since diseases like plague, cholera and many other were extensive and recurring taking heavy toll of people he opened a hospital in Kastur. A hospital was opened in Hadya also. Weekly clinics were arranged in few more villages. Later Sawday also embarked on leprosy eradication in some villages where that disease was found extensive. An Ashram for women was started in Kastur. Churches and parsonages were built in many villages.

Understandably, there were days without any rest for Sawday –ongoing construction works, buying of lands and sites, co-ordination, administration along with other regular missionary duties. He also had to spend a great deal of time in correspondence mainly writing appeals to friends and well wishers to collect funds for his various initiatives, in Mysore, CN area and other places.

When Sawday arrived in Mysore there was only one evangelist stationed in CN town/area. On the eve of his retirement in 1932 there were 16 evangelists busy working in villages of CN area! Indeed, what was taking place in CN villages had caught the attention far and wide, far beyond Mysore province, as a great inspiration and example.

Sawday- 'redeemer' of scores of children from slavery/Jitha

It was a shock for Sawday when he saw extensive practice of slavery (jitha) practice in villages of CN. He saw hundreds of people miserably entrapped in this most inhuman practice. He was especially deeply moved to see that children even of very tender age, as young as four years old were forced to be slave to the money lenders/land lords in lieu of debt made by their parents. Further Sawday discovered that quite a large number of children of newly converted families were also in slavery. Sawday being a person of great affection towards children could not hold back, any more. Redeeming of children from slavery and also mortgaged lands required huge amount of money. However, nothing deterred Sawday. The redemption of three children in Kastur in 1908 was the first case he had handled in CN villages. Soon after. scores of other cases were taken up in CN villages. Whenever he required money to redeem the enslaved children he would appeal to his friends and well wishers in England and India. Since all of them knew Sawday and his very dedicated work they used to overwhelmingly respond with their generous contributions. At times Sawday had to also use the District Loan Fund of the Mission to help to redeem the children.

A sustained support to redeemed slave children

Sawday's work never stopped with just redeeming the children who were in slavery. He gave a sustained support to those scores of children he had redeemed. He sent the redeemed children to boarding schools in Mysore and orphanages in Hassan and especially in Tumkur. Literally, hundreds of former slave children got a new lease of life in those boarding homes and orphanages finding access to education, vocational training and thus to a self supported life of freedom and human dignity. It would not be an exaggeration to say that hundreds of Christian families who now live in Bangalore, Mysore, CN villages and scores of other places in decent and respectable life are off spring of those former slave children who found a new lease of life. Such was Sawday's immemorial work.

The Mission report of 1922 gives a touching account of Sawday's work, on the eve of his departure on furlough. It stated:

After nine years without a break in the country, Mr. Sawday takes a long-deferred furlough this year. His praise is in all the churches here and at home. And not in the churches only, for on the suggestion we understand of his Highness the Maharaja the King-Emperor has been graciously pleased to award to him the Kaiser-i-Hind gold medal. We are all rejoicing at this public recognition of the great philanthropic work done by one whom we all love and respect so highly. Beloved by the many whom he has been the means of bringing to Christ, trusted by all his fellow-workers, and honoured by the King, we hope that he enjoy the happiest furlough he has ever known (MDR, 1922, p. 9).

Highlights of Sawday's other pioneering work

Apart from Sawday's monumental work in four areas as, briefly noted above, namely:

- Rehabilitation of scores of destitute children of Great Famine, Tumkur

- Pioneer Church Planter, especially in Chamarajanagara villages

- Master Builder of large number of major institutions of significance

- Especially in Mysore and CN circuits

- Redeemer of scores of children in jitha/slavery

There were other pioneering works where he made an indelible mark. They include, briefly:

1. Educational pioneer – God's chosen instrument in empowering the marginalized

Sawday started several schools in CN area and Mysore area. A taluk which was once steeped deep in illiteracy was greatly helped by the pioneer work of the mission through opening of many schools. It especially helped the literacy or education of the historically under privileged depressed classes, backward class people and women. Thus, the education work helped in the dawn of a new era or a new epoch in the land.

2.   Path breaking medical and community health work

Observing the recurring misery caused by plague, cholera, influenza Sawday took initiative to start hospitals in Mysore, Kastur (1923) and later in Hadya and dispensaries in some more villages. The hospital in Kastur became a well sought-after healing centre for all people in CN villages and far beyond.

3.   Pioneering work in leprosy eradication

Noticing the extensive problem of leprosy in parts of CN area Sawday initiated programme for prevention, and treatment of the disease. Those initiatives to prevent, treat and eradicate leprosy were first of their kind to be done in CN taluk, Mysore district. Thus, Sawday became pioneer of leprosy eradication in CN area, through his path breaking initiatives.

4.   Empowerment of women

The sight of countless problems faced by women in villages made Sawday to take various steps for their welfare. One of his most innovative initiatives was to start an Ashram for women in Kastur. The Ashram was called as Premalaya (abode of love). The Ashram consisted of a prayer room, a recreation room for women and babies and a house for sister in-charge of the Ashram. Sawday took great interest in this venture, raised funds and built it in 1925. He posted Sister Ethel Tomkinson as in-charge of the Ashram. Under her stewardship with the full support of Sawday, Premalaya flourished for years. Spiritual nurture and health awareness were two of the main concerns of her work among women. The fore sight of Sawday in establishing this Ashram is an indicator to the far-sighted vision of Sawday. Later a 'little (Chikka) Premalaya' was started in Hadya.

5.   Children, youth and women were Sawday's top priority, always

Sawday had carried a special concern as well as priority for children, youth and women in his ministry. In 1920 he stated, 'Hope of the churches lies in children and young people whom God has entrusted to our care' (MDR, 1920, p.68). In fact, his astounding work in Tumkur Orphanage during Great Famine time (1977-78), the entire educational work and his very remarkable work as redeemer of children in slavery were living witness for his concern.

6.   Temperance movement or campaign against alcoholism

Sawday saw that a large number of people in CN villages, especially men folk were addicted to alcohol drinks. Though living in abject poverty many of them had developed habitual drinking which not only ruined their own health but also of their families! This prompted Sawday to take up temperance movement or a campaign against drinking on a war footing. Be it in his preaching, teaching or exhortations, it became a regular thing to dissuade people from drinking. Further people were made to make pledge against drinking in writing. If they fail and break the pledge they had to pay a penalty which was not a small amount. This campaign was first initiated in Kastur and later extended to other villages. To dissuade people from hanging around toddy or arrack shops tea shops were being opened. The temperance campaign had noticeable success.

7.   Sawday – an advocate of freedom of religion

In Mysore province there was a law that if a person converts into another religion he forfeits all his/her property rights, inheritance and even right over his own children. Ironically majority of Hindu and even Muslim community believed that such a law was good and opposed to any change in it. However, the Wesleyan missionaries as well as representatives of other Christian denominations felt that it was a serious violation of human rights and of freedom of religion. They also thought that it was a serious obstacle for people to convert into Christianity. Missionaries along with the representatives of other Christian denominations constantly appealed for revision of this law. However, though Mysore Maharaja was very sympathetic to the appeal of the missionaries the majority community was rigid and did not give any chance for a revision. Sawday was a persistent advocate of abolition of the oppressive Act.

8.   Sawday – an outstanding crusader against caste

From the very beginning Sawday was totally opposed to caste, be it within the church or within the society at large. His entire ministry, preaching, teaching and the ministry had that basic foundation of a perception which uncompromisingly opposed to caste. Sawday, perceived caste as polar opposite to Gospel. His position on caste was very similar to the stance of all the Protestant Missions working in India at that time.

9.   Sawday-a highly placed churchman in church/ Mission governance

Sawday was an outstanding churchman who was repeatedly entrusted with or elevated to high position in Mission/Church administration. He had carved out a niche for himself with a distinct and respected position not only in the Mysore provincial circle but also in the global Wesleyan Mission circle. It was very striking that he was made as the Chairman of the Provincial Synod of the Wesleyan Mission twice in 1904 and 1928. Adding to this he was repeatedly chosen as acting Chairman of the Synod six times namely, in 1902, 1907, 1914-1922, 1927, and 1930. That was a rare honor bestowed on Sawday. It tells of the great esteem with which Sawday was being held in the church governance in Mysore province and far beyond in the Wesleyan Methodist fraternity.

Sawday was elected to 'Legal Hundred' which was a unique honor bestowed on him within the Methodist Church.

10. Sawday- an ardent supporter of ministerial/seminary training and literature work

Further apart from the above noted institutions Sawday also strongly supported/promoted many initiatives of far reaching impact.

They include

- A theological training institute attached to Hardwicke School which was functioning in Mysore from 1879. This Theological institute was later shifted to Bangalore, named as United Theological College and became an all India institution much repute. Sawday promoted such institutions actively.

- In 1923 a women's Bible training centre started in Tumkur Seminary. Sawday was one of the prominent supporters of this initiative.

- 'Vruthantha Pathrike': This Kannada weekly paper was started by the Wesleyan missionary Henry Haigh in 1887 and had become a widely circulated news journal in the entire Mysore region. Sawday and Tomlinson were active supporters and patrons of this work. The paper however ceased to publish in 1941, unable to bear the competition.

More examples of Sawday's innovative work

- In CN villages he started **"Jholam Fund"** in the congregations. The objective of the fund was to raise redemption money from within the congregations so as to redeem the slave children in Christian families.

- There are references in Wesleyan Mission reports that two **co-operative societies** were started in CN villages (MDR, 1940, p.12). The objective of the society was to stop people from being caught in debt trap. However more details about this initiative are not available.

- As part of economic self empowerment training in **mat -making** was arranged in villages.

- To encourage and support the higher education of CN boys and girls Sawday established Higher **Education Scholarship Fund** which helped many young men and women in their post-metric education.

- Further Sawday established huge fund to pay **pension to the retired pastors.** This is called as Sawday Pension Fund and greatly helping even today to pay pension to retired pastors of all three dioceses of CSI in Karnataka.

Universal recognition to Sawday's work

Sawday was awarded 'Kaisar-i-Hind' gold medal (first class) from the British crown in 1923. The award was given on the recommendation of Maharaja of Mysore for his meritorious public service. Sawday was held in high respect both in palace and in the public.

In 1937 Sawday was made as a Member of the Constitutional Reform Committee of Mysore province.

He was held in great esteem by the Mysore Royal family and had a close contact with the Maharaja. It was due this special relationship Mysore kings extended much support to many Mission work such as hospital, schools etc.

When Nalvadi Krisharaja Wodeyar passed away in 1940 it was Sawday who had the rare honor to preside over the public condolence meeting held in Bangalore.

The Mysore city council had named one prominent road in Mandi Mohalla of Mysore as Sawday Street, as a tribute to the outstanding work of this servant of God.

There are over a dozen of churches in Chamarajanagara villages and many more in Mysore, Bangalore, Mandya and Tumkur which today carry the name 'Sawday Memorial Church', a very rare honor to the legendary missionary.

Post-retirement days of Sawday

Sawday retired from active service in 1932. He was in service for 56 years, all of it in Mysore province. After retirement in 1932 Sawday went to England, however since he had decided to make India as his home he returned back to his much beloved Mysore city in 1933. Although retired from active service he continued to actively help in the affairs of the Mission. He especially continued very much involving in the continuing expansion work of Holdsworth Memorial Hospital.

The octogenarian Sawday's advice was often sought after within the churches and in the Mission circle.

Sawday continued to be very close to Wodeyar and the Mysore Royal family.

Sawday in his 44 years of stay in Mysore i.e. from the year of his arrival in 1900 to his year of demise in 1944, only three times he visited England on furlough, for short periods. He took furlough in 1912, 1922 and 1933.

In 1933 when Kastur church celebrated its Silver Jubilee, Sawday was very much there participating in the grand celebration. Tomlinson was the main preacher on the occasion.

In 1937 Sawday visited Tumkur for the opening of a new school adjoining the orphanage. It was an event taking place after 60 years since the orphanage started in 1877 during the Great Famine time when Sawday was a young missionary of just 23 years age. The 60th anniversary/diamond anniversary event was very memorable. Interestingly 33 gray haired famine orphan boys, admitted in 1877, were present in the event (MDR, 1937, p.25). In 1937 Sawday was made a Member of the Constitutional Reform Committee of Mysore province, an honour, bestowed for his distinguished statesmanship.

During the second half of 1930s Sawday became busy with yet another construction, an 'occupation' which was so dear to the heart of this master builder. A maternity ward was built in Holdsworth Memorial Hospital and opened in 1938. It was Sawday's initiative and financially also he was the main supporter (Sargant, 48).

In 1938 when Kastur church celebrated its 30th anniversary Sawday was very much present on that occasion.

The Mysore Maharaja Nalvadi Krishnaraja Wodeyar passed away in 1940. As noted earlier, Sawday had the rare honour of presiding over the public condolence meeting held in Bangalore. Sawday paid rich tributes to Wodeyar for his tolerance, compassion and reformed governance (MDR, 1940, pp.3-4).

On August 31, 1941 Sawday was in Tumkur, again. He laid the foundation for churches in Bethelur and Devanur, two Christian villages which he himself established during the Great Famine period six decades ago. Sawday also participated in the 60th anniversary of Wesley Church, Tumkur (Sargant, p 52).

Last days of Sawday
In the meanwhile, Sawday's health condition was steadily turning frail. He had to increasingly confine to his home. The responsibilities of Mysore and CN circuits were now on the shoulders of Tomlinson, Sargant, Gurushantha and other ministers.

Sawday celebrated his 90th birthday in March 1944
The year 1944 turned out to be a year of great loss. First it was the untimely death of Lily Lamech daughter of Sawday's very close associate/friend, Rev. Samuel Lamech. She was the principal of the noted Wesleyan institute, Victoria School in Mysore. In 1944 Sister F.E. Campbell passed away. Next it was Rev. Tomlinson's turn. He was a very close associate of Sawday in Mysore and Chamarajanagara work for many years. Tomlinson's end came suddenly. He died while playing tennis in Mysore on August 29, 1944.

By this time Sawday was becoming very frail. He had met with an accident in February 1944 from which he did not fully recover. At this juncture the Mission arranged Sister Ethel Tomkinson of Premalaya in Kastur to take care of the bed- ridden Sawday. She took care of the ailing Sawday for six months (MDR, 1944, p.10).

Sawday breathed his last on 16th September 1944.
From 1876, the year of his arrival to India Sawday served 18 years in Tumkur/area, 6 years he was working in England (1894-1900) and the last 44 for years until his death he lived in Mysore, an

unsurpassing record indeed. There was a great concourse of people from all walks of life gathered to pay him their last respect. The Mysore palace had sent its special police to the funeral to pay the final respects. His coffin was carried by men who were once redeemed by Sawday from slavery. The coffin was carried through the streets of Mysore city and was buried in Bartholomew's Cemetery. Sawday's tomb lies in the same row where Tomlinson was also laid to rest.

CHAPTER-10

Chronology of Events

Wesleyan Mission Work
in Mysore Province
Focus on: Chamarajanagara Area

1703 Birth of John Wesley in England, the pioneer of Methodist Movement.

1799 Fall of Tippu Sultan on 4th May 1799. Wodeyar family re-instated as Mysore kings, under British authority.

1811 Mummadi Krishnaraja Wodeyar becomes Maharaja of Mysore province at the age of 16.

1812 Founding of Methodist Mission in UK under the leadership of Dr. Thomas Coke. British Parliament constitutionally approves Christian Mission work in India. Dr. Thomas Coke 'Father of Wesleyan Methodist Mission' embarks on a missionary voyage to India but died in the sea.

1817 Wesleyan missionary James Lynch starts working in Madras.

1819   Rev. James Lynch writes to Home Committee stating that the Wesleyan Mission could start work in Mysore Province since facilities available.

1821   Rev. Elijah Hoole the first Wesleyan Missionary to Mysore Province arrives in Bangalore on 29th April. The second Missionary Rev. James Mowat arrives in June. They started working among the English and the Tamils.

1824   Hoole transferred to Madras and Mowat to Nagapatnam. Mission work in Mysore province temporarily discontinued.

1825   Madras District of Wesleyan Mission constituted; until then the Mission work was part of Ceylon District.

1831   Political transition- Mysore province transferred from Maharaja to British Resident Commissioner.

1833   Wesleyan Missionary Thomas Hodson was transferred from Calcutta to Bangalore. He started working among English and Tamils.

1834   Home Committee directs missionaries in Bangalore to focus more on Kanarese Work/people.

1835   Wesleyan missionaries in Bangalore request the Home Committee to send four men to work among Kannada people.

1836   Thomas Hodson embarks on a long round trip to explore the possibility of opening Mission stations.

1837   Hodson establishes first mission station in Gubbi, in the central part of Mysore Province.

1838   Hodson opens mission stations at Kunigal and Mysore.

1839   A Kanarese Circuit constituted within Madras District which greatly helped the work among Kannada people. A printing press started in Bangalore. This was closed in 1873 and later re-started in Mysore. Mission purchases a bungalow from Wodeyars in Mysore.

1840   Three schools started in Mysore; pupils admitted without caste or gender Discrimination.

1841   First congregation of Wesleyan Mission was formed in Bangalore. It was a Tamil church.

1843   First conversion of a Kannadiga in December 1843, in Gubbi. Chikka (after baptism Daniel) was a young washer man.

1844   A girls' boarding school started in Mysore.

1848   Mysore District of Wesleyan Mission was constituted. Up to that time the work was under Madras District. In 1848 total members in Wesleyan congregations were 38, mostly Tamils.

1854   Wesleyan Mission school started. In 1892 renamed as Hardwicke High School.

1857   Sepoy Mutiny. End of East India Company rule and beginning of British Crown Rule.

1876   Rev. George William Sawday arrived in India. His first station Kunigal.

1877   The 'Great Famine' in south India. Wesleyan Mission actively joins in relief work. Canarese Orphanage started in Tumkur. Sawday transferred to Tumkur.

1878   Rev. Thomas Hodson retires and returns to England.

1879   Sawday becomes in-charge of the work in Gubbi, Tumkur and Kunigal. Wesleyan missionaries' first visit to Chamarajanagara. Rev. Abijah Samuel, first Kannada pastor passed away.

1881   The administration of Mysore Province was transferred to Wodeyars, again.

1882   Hodson, 'Father of Mysore Mission', dies in England.

1885   A Mission station started in Chamarajanagara town with Bhakti Siromoni as evangelist.

1886   A Mission worship centre developed in Chamarajanagara.

1887   Rev. Henry Haigh started weekly paper, 'Vruthantha Pathrike' in Mysore.

1888   Wesleyan Mission starts a girl's school in Ramasamudram and an English school in Chamarajanagara town.

1889   First two Wesleyan Mission converts in CN town, a woman and a Soliga man.

1890   CN town congregation has six full members and few children.

1894   Nalvadi Krishnaraja Wodeyar becomes the ruler of Mysore Province. He was the ruler until his death in 1940.

1895   A Mission school started in Nagavelli village, 15 kms east of CN town.

1898   A school started at weavers' colony in CN town.

1900   Sawday posted to Mysore, on his return from England Devastating plague and famine in CN area.

1903   Victoria School started in Mysore.

1906   Holdsworth Hospital started in Mysore. Calvert Boarding School opened in Mysore

1908   Beginning of 'Kastur movement' with conversion of Mudda (Abraham) and Mada (Devadas). Sawday baptizes 8 adults and 5 children in Kastur. Baptisms in Bhogapura.

1909   Conversions in M. Hosur.

1910   Conversions in Homma. District Evangelistic Band started with Rev. W.E. Tomlinson as the leader.

1915   Baptisms in Madigahalli (Madapura) Sawday was awarded Kaiser-e-Hind award by the British Crown.

1920   M.K. Gandhi takes on leadership of national freedom movement.

1921   Centenary of Wesleyan Mission in Mysore province celebrated.

1922   Kastur Mission hospital opened with Dr. P. Yesudas as doctor.

1923   Maharajah gives 5 seats to Christian community in State Admi. Council.

1925   An Ashram for women 'Premalaya' started in Kastur.

1932   Sawday retires. Rev. Tomlinson builds Tumkur Seminary Church in Chalukya style.

1933   Kastur Church celebrates Silver Jubilee. A hospital opened in Hadya. Dr. V.Abraham made in charge.

1936   Baptisms in Mudnakod. A Mission House built in CN town.

1937   Intensive Leprosy work around Talwadi region Sawday was made as member of Constitutional Reform Committee of Mysore provincial government.

1939   A congregation started in Mettluvadi. An anti conversion bill was placed before the State Council but did not become a law.

1940   Death of Krishnaraja Wodeyar. Jayachamarajendra Wodeyar succeeds as King.

1941   A Wesleyan Synod Commission visits CN area. 'Vruthantha Pathrike' news paper closed down unable to bear the competition

1942   Congregations in Tiganare, Gajanur and T. Hosur started. Rev. L Jonathan. K. Shadrach and Kenchappa all three pioneer evangelists of CN area passed away. Quit India Movement

1943   Baptisms in Karalavadi and Kottanahalli villages of Talwadi region.

1944   New station in Talavadi opened. Death of Tomlinson on 29th August. Death of Sawday on 16th September.

1947   India got Independence CSI was inaugurated. Wesleyan congregations in Mysore Province became part of undivided Mysore Diocese. Rev. P. Gurushantha of Mysore was consecrated as the first Bishop of Mysore Diocese.

PART - B

A Glimpse to the Present Socio-economic Condition of Christians in Chamarajanagara Villages

Linking pre-1947 to the present

In linking with CSI period beginning from 1947 to the present few important mile stones may be noted:

- *When CSI was inaugurated in September 1947 all the Wesleyan congregations including those in CN area became part of the united church namely CSI. The founding of CSI, a historic event was welcomed with much rejoice and hope.*

- *With the inauguration of CSI former Wesleyan congregations in Mysore province became part of the erstwhile undivided CSI Mysore Diocese.*

- *A Wesleyan minister Premaka Gurushantha was consecrated in 1947 as the first Bishop of the undivided Mysore Diocese of CSI. Gurushantha who had many years of pastoral work experience in Mysore and Bangalore areas was son of a veteran minister Premaka who among other places had labored many years in CN villages.*

- *Norman C. Sargant, a Wesleyan missionary who had long experience of working in Mysore province including in CN circuit was consecrated as the second Bishop of Undivided Mysore Diocese in 1951, succeeding Bishop Gurushantha.*

- *On 1ˢᵗ May 1970 after several months of deliberation the undivided Mysore Diocese was trifurcated in to three Dioceses namely Karnataka Southern Diocese, Karnataka Central Diocese and Karnataka Northern Diocese with their headquarters in Mangalore, Bangalore and Dharwad, respectively.*

The former Wesleyan congregations in erstwhile districts of Mysore province except Bangalore, Tumkur, KGF, Shimoga and Chitradurga, all came under the jurisdiction of Karnataka Southern Diocese (KSD) with its headquarters in Mangalore. The congregations of CN area also became part of the KSD.

- *The KSD constituted mainly former Wesleyan congregations as noted above and the former Basel Mission congregations of undivided Dakshina Kannada and Coorg districts.*

- Sabestian *Rathnakara Furtado (Mangalore) was consecrated as the Bishop of the newly formed KSD in 1971. The Diocese consisted of an estimated 60% former Basel Mission Christians and 40% Wesleyan Methodist Christians*

- *Subsequent to Furtado four others became the Bishop of KSD, all from former Basel Mission background. The present Bishop of KSD Mohan Manoraj hails from Kastur in CN district, credited to be the first one to become the Bishop of KSD from the former Wesleyan Methodist Church/area.*

- *Seven decades have passed since the CN congregations became part of CSI, and five decades completed ever since they became part of CSI-KSD. Many pioneers had labored in this district and number of initiatives was taken up to help the growth of congregations/ Christian community in the area. However, a general feeling of dismay about the inadequate progress of the community and growth of the church is continuing to linger in the minds of many who were genuinely concerned to see rejuvenated and growing churches in CN area.*

- *The purpose of the survey conducted by this writer in the CN area during 20-30 October 2016, was precisely aimed to find out possible obstacles which hinder the growth of the churches and the progress of the community.*

The Living Condition of Christians in CN area today

Habitat

In Indian villages usually people belonging to different castes reside in different localities of village. This is because traditionally caste is the basis of Indian society and it continues to have a hold on the social behavior of people. If upper and dominant caste people generally reside in the central locations of village, the backward communities (OBC) live in adjacent area at the back. The depressed class people reside on the periphery or outskirt of village. By and large this is the scenario in most villages, from time unknown.

The C N villages are not different in this matter. Brahmins, if any of their family still live in the village and the Lingayats occupy the central area of village. Next to them OBC/Shudra communities have their residential localities. Generally, while more dominant OBC community live closer to the central location of village, poorer OBC/ Shudra communities live in the borders. As far as the depressed class families are concerned, whether they are 'Hindu' or are Christians, live in the periphery of village. Usually the Christian prayer sheds/churches and parsonages are also located around this locality of the village.

Housing

A majority of Christian families live in tin or country made tile roof huts/houses

Christian houses used to be mostly thatched huts reflecting their poor socio-economic condition. Like Christians, most of the other depressed class and poorer backward community people also used to live mostly in thatched huts. As far as the upper/dominant caste families were concerned most lived in country made tile roof houses. To live in country made tile house was a 'luxury' in olden days and usually only economically sound families could afford it.

However, the times have changed. The thatched huts were being replaced by tin sheet and country made tile roof houses. In much recent times Mangalore tile roof houses and concrete houses are increasing in number, especially with families which are economically better placed. This change over the years has taken place in Christian community too. In our Sample survey we found that out of 348 Christian families reported:

Living in thatched huts	1.4%
Tin sheet houses	19%
Country made tile houses	40%
Mangalore tile houses	31%
Concrete houses	9%

The above table is self-explanatory and it points out to a few facts clearly:

1. Number of Christian families living in thatch-huts almost fully reduced.

2. Families living in hutments and tin sheet and country made tile roof houses almost amount to 60%. These houses or

huts are generally in congested residential places with little or no proper ventilation. The huts/houses are very fragile and vulnerable to extreme weather conditions such as heavy rain fall, high mercury level etc. The above table points out to the reality that nearly 2/3 of all Christian families in CN villages live in such shelter in CN villages. This is an important indicator pointing to the poor economic condition of Christians.

3. Thirty one percent live in Mangalore tile houses and 9% in cement/concrete houses making 40% altogether. These houses are little larger and have a better ventilation. Obviously, the economic condition of these 40% is relatively better, but not fully free from financial struggles.

Loans from different sources helped upgrading their huts/houses

The soft loan availed from government through banks and societies helped quite many families to re-construct or repair their own huts/houses or even helped them to build a new one. Therefore, they could change from tin roof houses to Mangalore tiles or even concrete houses. It was found that among those who availed loan as high as 39% of families made the loan for the housing purpose only.

In some cases, the migrant members of the family too financially supported the repair or reconstruction of their family houses.

Drinking Water

Perennial scarcity of water- Christians quite often subjected to caste abuse at wells/water points

Scarcity of drinking water is a major problem in CN villages.

True, in most places village panchayats have constructed water storage tanks, bore well and water points in different residential localities of village. Christians too have either bore well or water taps in their residential localities provided by Panchayat.

However, during long summer season and drought times, when water tap/bore wells dry up people under go untold misery. They run from one bore wells to other in search of water. Since under-water level usually gets depleted in the entire region practically everyone suffer, people, livestock and entire agricultural activity.

A century ago when Sawday began work in CN area, after seeing people's misery, one of the first things he did was to dig wells. There were as many as 15 wells reportedly dug in villages because of Sawday's initiative. However, all those wells have now either sunk or become totally unusable.

People suffer untold difficulties during the time of water scarcity. The poorer section of the village suffers worst during those acute water crisis days. Christians (as well other depressed class people) go to bore wells located in caste Hindu localities with the hope of drawing a little water from there. However, they are not welcomed at well or bore well located at caste Hindu localities. It was reported that usually the Lingayat people show maximum contempt on Christians and depressed class people, at the water points. Often, they are subjected to much casteist humiliation on those occasions.

During the time of acute water crisis people are forced to tread long distances to fetch a little water from a stream or pond. Usually women and children do this job of fetching water, often walking those long distances under hot sun. Even if they succeed in collecting a pot of water what they collect is usually not potable one but potentially one which causes water- borne diseases.

Electricity

Majority of the families have free power connection; but the power cut is always very acute

An overwhelming majority of Christian families reported that their huts/houses are connected with electricity. Those who reported that they had no electric connection were surprisingly very few. Two points may be briefly noted here, first, the fact that most Christian families in spite of their abject poverty own electric facility. andmost families do not pay for the power consumption but avail it freely under some government scheme. Secondly in spite of the claim by the government about an increased power production, most of the villages still suffer from acute power scarcity. This is the story of CN area also. In fact only for a few hours of the day power is being supplied to rural areas. Obviously the power supply condition is worst during summer days.

Toilet

Majority of families claim to be having a semblance of toilet in their huts/houses

It was reported that most of the Christian households have their own toilet facility within their houses. In a condition where a majority of families still live in congested little tin or country tile huts/houses the claim of having toilet facility naturally raises doubts. However, on cross checking this fact it was found that the reportwas true. While some people go out to the open place for toilet purpose it appears most families have made their own arrangements within their houses. This in fact shows people's better sanitary sense which is appreciable.

Family

Family Pattern

More nuclear families - joint families fast decreasing

Following family pattern was discovered among Christians in CN area:

Nuclear	71%
Extended	19%
Joint	10%

A brief note is required to define the terms used above. A 'nuclear' family means a family with a couple (husband and wife) and their un-married children, living under one roof. 'Extended' means besides a couple and children a widowed mother or father or unmarried brother/sister also living together. A' joint' family means besides a couple and their children one or more couples also living under one roof.

It is very clear that the Christian community even in rural area is fast adapting to nuclear pattern of family, which is generally a common trend in urban areas, since long. This trend is so pervasive that according to our data out of 26 CN villages in as high as 11 villages no trace of joint families was found at all. In a few villages all families were found to be just only nuclear (Kerehalli, Talwadi and Karalavadi).

Christian families becoming increasingly smaller

Christian families in CN villages are small in size. The average number of persons in a nuclear family is four, which includes parents plus two children. In fact there are many Christian families with only single child. It appears that the time of traditional joint families and couples having 4-5 children is over. Various compulsions and factors especially economic factors played a role in this change with an enhanced awareness and media impact also contributing to the change. Multiple factors have influenced people to go for smaller family.

Alarming number of widows in the community

A matter of concern is the large number of widows found in Christian families in CN area. Out of 205 female respondents (total respondents 360 in 26 villages) as high as 63 women were found to be widows. This is indeed an alarming number. Out of those 63 widows 14 were found to be in the age group of 35 to 60 years.

While the number of widows were found to be alarmingly higher in the community, the number of widowers were found to be very small. It was found out that out of 155 male respondents (total respondents 360 in 26 villages) there were only 7 widowers. Compare this with number of widows which is 63. The large disparity between the number of widows and the number of widowers should raise some serious concern as well as questions.

Pathetic condition in which most widows live

The large number of widows in the Christian community and their pathetic condition points out to some hard realities in the Christian community which include:

1) Most of the widows were found to be landless, illiterate or semi –literate, without any life support. They are mostly aged and disabled to eke out a living on their own. It was found that aged widows, as old as in 70s and 80s, work in the fields as coolies for a pittance of a coolie of just Rs.100/ per day, for their survival. This was a pathetic scene.

2) It was discovered that while some widows lived in families, a larger number of widows lived all alone with no one to take care.

3) In some cases widows' migrant family members living afar support the widow back in the village. However many times there was no support extended. On the whole it was discovered that widows are left in a lurch to suffer all their physical, financial and emotional agonies on their own.

Remarriage of widows–a taboo

It was found that the widows in CN villages were mostly of 60-70 years old. But there were also a good number of widows in 40s and 50s. Whatever their age, re-marriage of women remain a taboo or an unacceptable thing, a problem men folk generally did not face.

Majority of widows do not get widows' pension–lack of awareness and of persons to properly guide

Out of 63 widows,only 15 widows in our Sample were found to be availing widow's pension from the State. A great lack of awareness in the community was very much evident. Adding to this there is lack of helping hands within the community who would give the necessary information and help in applying for the pension.

For many of the widows, widow's pension is the only life support, for which those hapless women wait month after month, eagerly. Presently widow's pension is Rs.500/ pm.

Aged and disabled couples living all alone–Effect of migration and nuclearisation of families

Yet another hard reality found in the CN area is the alarming number of aged and disabled couples living all alone.

This author recollects how a lecturer now retired and settled in Bangalore lamented about his native CN district, 'My district has become a large old age home, now' This exclamation concurs well when during the course of the field study an unusual number of aged/disabled couples were found living all alone, in many villages. It appears that rapid migration of most of the able-bodied people from villages, growing nuclearisation and a chronic famine stricken condition in the land have all contributed to this pathetic condition of the widows and the old age people in the area.

Deplorable condition of aged couples, living all alone

Needless to state that most of those aged couples are illiterates or semi literates and most are also landless. True, some of them own small pieces of land but as in the case of most of the CN Christian families those pieces of land are mostly dry land, the cultivation of which depends on erratic/unpredictable rain fall. In other words the pieces of land they own are not productive. Under this circumstance many aged couple forced to work as coolies. It is a very pathetic scene to see how men and women in their 70s and 80s are slogging as daily wage coolies for a wage of Rs.150/ for male and 100/ for female. True in few cases the migrated member (s) of the family does support the aged parents but in many cases either their support is nil or the support is very irregular.

It was discovered that a few aged couples succeeded in availing old age pension from the State which is Rs, 500/ per month. However the number of such beneficiaries is very small in CN area. In fact in most villages old aged couple do not avail this state benefit of old age pension. Lack of awareness as well as helping hand to assist the aged appears to be the basic problem.

Educational Condition

Wesleyan Mission legacy

Thanks for the legacy of Wesleyan Mission's remarkable educational work in CN villages, which greatly helped in the progress of the land. If today a majority of Christians in the area is literate and even succeeded in reaching/ finishing metric level the credit goes to the strong educational basis laid by the Wesleyan missionaries. True, university level and professional degree holders are very minimal in the community. Their poor economic condition was the main cause behind why many could not pursue education beyond metric level.

The invaluable labour of Wesleyan Mission in making a historically suppressed and backward people literate is a great saga of faith. On the one hand Mission opened schools in CN villages and opened their doors for women, depressed class and backward class people. On the other hand it opened boarding homes and schools and vocational centres in Mysore, Hassan and Tumkur and sent scores of boys and girls from CN villages to those institutions. That gave a new lease of life to those children. Truly the educational endeavor of Wesleyan Mission had a catalytic effect on the people, although it is still a long way to go.

Educational level of respondents - A quarter is illiterate-- majority under metrics

The findings of Sample study point out to the following educational level of respondents who were altogether 360 in number in 26 villages of CN area (male 155, female 205).

Following is the educational level of respondents:

Illiterate	24%
Primary level (1-3 classes)	6%

Higher Primary (4-7 classes)   20%
High school (8-10 Classes)   26%
Pre-University (11-12 classes)   19%
Graduate & Post graduate level 5%

The above statistics from the Sample survey also broadly reflects the educational condition of adult Christian community in CN. With reference to the above table it may be noted that,

1. Twenty four percent of the respondents were found to be illiterate. As per the Indian Census 2011 reports 39% of CN district population is illiterate while the state percentage of illiterates is 25%. This indicates the Christian community in CN stands considerably better in literacy level compared to CN district population.

2. The percentage of college level education is minimal with 5% among the respondents. It appears that a good number of people somehow manage to reach up to secondary level of education but post metric/university level education becomes a distant dream for most of them. Needless to say, that it is mainly their poor economic condition which hinders Christian youth to pursue higher education.

Variations in educational level–Madapura and Kastur congregations' score higher achievement

It was found that there is great variation in educational achievement of CN Christians, from village to village. While villages like Madapura and Kastur have gained a remarkable higher educational achievement, in most of the other villages, especially of Talwadi region, educational level lags behind very much.

The one Ph.D student who was found in the course of this survey was in Madapura, a village, as noted earlier, had achieved a higher educational achievement.

A few striking features of Christian community as related to educational condition may be further noted here below:

1. Most mission schools now closed

Once there were as many as nine Mission schools during 1944-47, in CN villages, providing education to children of all sections of the population be they were caste Hindus, Scheduled castes, Scheduled tribes, women and of course to children of the neo converts families. This was in pre independence period. Unable to bear the exorbitant establishment charges and the competition from mushrooming English medium/private schools almost all the Mission schools were closed, one by one, long ago. Presently only two Mission schools, one in Kastur and the other in CN Town are functioning, though very feebly.

2. Rapidly growing motivation for children's education.

Child labourers and school drop outs are fewer in the community

It was found that Christian parents are very keen to send their children to school. The Sample survey found few cases of illiterate children in the community. Further instances of school dropout children and child laborers were also not many. Whatever the odds may be by and large most of parents were found to be keen to send their children to school.

3. Parents increasingly dream to send their children to English medium schools

Today English medium schools and residential schools are mushrooming in CN area also, including in villages. Most Christians, like the rest, very much aspire to send their children to English medium schools. But the high cost of education in those schools hinders most of them. In spite of this hoping that their children will have a better future one day, a small segment of Christian community do struggle to send children to English medium school only.

4. More interest on College education- but poverty does not allow

Just as CN village Christians show increasing motivation for their children schooling, many of them carry much interest for their college education too. However the abject poverty of many or the limited economic resource stands as a big obstacle for the dream of college education.

5. People are quite literate/educated, but majority are unemployed or under employed

A striking number of youth and middle age men and women though completed metric level or even degree level of education discovered to be either unemployed or under employed. In this context 'under employed' means not engaged in a job which does not match their educational qualification. A large number of men especially in the age group of 20-40 though completed metric or even degree level found to be working as coolies, electricians, painters, bus conductors and basic computer workers. It is a frustrating situation. The condition of educated women especially those who were in their young or middle age found to be even more depressing. While most of them were found to be unemployed, many in their despair found to be working as coolies and garment workers. More about this will be explained in a subsequent section.

6. Few main reasons for unemployment/under employment–lack of awareness, financial resource and communal prejudice/harassment.

The problem of educated unemployment and under employment is not new to India. CN Christians point out several reasons behind this situation in their area. The reason they sight include: lack of reservation, communal prejudice and harassment, lack of awareness and lack of sufficient drive among people in highly competitive context. People do not fail to point out that the failure of the church/leadership in creating awareness among the people about the opportunities available was also a basic problem.

7. Girls out beat boys in general education and higher education

It was found that girls are doing very well not only at school level but also at college level. Few decades ago girls were lagging much behind boys mainly because of the gender inequality with regard to education. But this scenario is fast changing now.

In the Sample it was found that out of 81 graduates in the community 36 were female and 45 male. This means that the girls were much close to boys and competing in pursuing college education.

Further it was found that at the PG level girls out beat boys Out of 22 PGs found in the Sample 12 were female and 10 males.

8. **The dire need of vocational/job oriented training and encouragement for professional courses.**

It was discovered that in CN area those who were trained in different trades got job opportunities relatively easier than others. For example those who after metric level had their training in ITI, CSI Vocational Centre found job as electrician, mechanic, carpenters etc. In the same way the girls who were trained in Para- medical courses got job as lab technicians, nurses, etc, relatively easier.

Respondents time and again repeatedly appealed that the church leadership should understand the very difficult economic condition in CN area and embark on imparting job oriented or vocational training to Christian youth, on a very urgent basis. Only such training carries greater certainty of assuring young men and even women a livelihood and thus could empower the community. The respondents pleaded that such training centers should be set up in the area urgently on a priority basis.

It may be recollected that around 1940s the Wesleyan Mission was seriously thinking of setting up of a vocational training centre in Heggewadi in CN area. They felt the urgency of such a centre mainly on two grounds: first, the urgent need to impart trade training to youth and thus to socio-economically empower the community. Secondly they felt that the CSI vocational training centre in Tumkur was over burdened and therefore to relieve it a new centre in Heggewadi was desirable. It is unfortunate however that the proposed project which would have become a great boon to CN area never became a reality at all.

Encouraging and supporting youth for professional courses and competitive exams is also an urgent need in CN area. There are hardly any engineering, medical, law and such other professional studies under taken by Christian youth in CN area.

9. CN Christians repeated appeal with the Diocese to help them to their children's education.

It may be noted that as much as people's motivation for their children's education was growing equally also their persistence that the church/Diocese should support children's education. In fact this plea was echoed all over the CN area, in almost all the 26 villages where the Sample survey was conducted. People demand that the church should mainly work on following four programs:

1. Provide regular scholarship to all children studying.

2. Open all mission schools which were closed. Set up new boarding homes and schools in CN area including for college level.

3. Establish job oriented/vocational training centres in CN area.

4. Establish job oriented training centres for women, urgently.

Economic condition

Christians- part of poor population in villages

In most of CN Villages Christians belong to the poorest of the poor section of the population. They are in the bottom line by every parameter. Christians are aware of this fact and they painfully acknowledge the reality. Their condition is almost same as the other depressed class people. At least the 'Hindu' Dalits have SC reservation provision and constitutional protection but Christians have none. True, many backward or OBC communities also live in extreme poverty and illiteracy as Christians do. But they are 'touchables' and as such they do not suffer the social degradation which 'Hindu' Dalits and Christians suffer.

Occupations of village Christians

Majority of Christians in agricultural occupations

It was discovered that 50 to 60% of all Christian families are engaged in agricultural occupation. This percentage is likely to reduce further. According to Census 2011 in CN district 68% of the families are engaged in agricultural occupation.

It was noticed that while in some villages a larger number of families still dependent on agriculture occupations, in few villages there was a rapid tilt toward non-agricultural occupations among families.

Majority of Christians are coolies and marginal farmers

Those engaged in agricultural occupations may be classified into three categories. They are:

1. **Coolies:** They are mostly land less families. They eke out their livelihood working in fields belonging to village land lords. While in some villages like Kastur, Madapura and Hadya the men coolies get Rs. 500/ as daily wage in most other villages the daily wage ranges between rupees 200 to 300/ only. With the cost of living gone sky high the daily wage is hardly sufficient to support families and to live a decent life. Further during famine time which is a recurring phenomenon in the area, the agricultural activities come to a standstill and people find it extreme difficult to secure even a day's coolie work. This is an inexplicably miserable time for the poorest of the village.

2. **Marginal Farmers:** These people possess small pieces of land, about 1 to 3 acres, mostly 'dry' land with cultivation dependant entirely on scarce/erratic rain fall. Since the land they posses is small they cannot financially sustain the family. This forces many of them to work as agricultural coolies, in other people's fields.

3. **Farmers:** This is relatively a smaller segment among CN Christians. Generally they hold 4 to 6 acres of land. Few of the lands were 'wet' ones, which mean little more productive land. Generally those families manage to support their families. Besides if one or two from the families engaged in non-agricultural occupation their condition could be somewhat comfortable. True, during the drought season these families too suffer, but their economic condition is relatively better than the majority in their community.

Growing number of Christians go for non-agricultural occupations

The compelling conditions of CN area are driving an increasing number of people to non-agricultural occupations. Today many village Christians are found in varied occupations other than agriculture. While some work in their own villages or in nearby larger villages, many work in places like CN town and Nanjanagudu. Some even work in Mysore city and they daily commute, to and fro.

Further while some of the non-agricultural occupations are skilled most other are unskilled ones. Since by and large Christians are average educated which means achieved under metric or metric level education at the most only, the job they are engaged also reflect an average level.

Most common non- agricultural occupations among Christians

Majority are in unskilled and skilled labour

Electrician, driver, carpenter, tailor, mason, painter, plumber, mechanic, lab technician, basic computer work, silk work, petty shop, or small business, nomadic seller, peon in schools and offices, security guards, garment work, auto driver, shop or show room sales boy, sales executive, panchayat office assistant, brick work, concrete work/ contract, granite work, decoration work, florist, music artist, poultry, cow, sheep and goat rearing, dairy and so on.

Occupations in which Christians are found in fewer number:

Office clerk, teachers, nurses, lecturers etc. In professions like engineers, medical doctors, lawyers, officer levels Christians were rarely found.

Women in non-agricultural occupations

As noted earlier most of the women were found either unemployed or under employed. Few women were found in occupations like nurse, teacher, nursery/anganawadi helper, ayah, lab-technician, garment, and dairy and so on.

Wage pattern of agricultural coolies

Big variations–gross gender inequality

As noted earlier a large number of Christians, both men and women work as agricultural coolies in CN area. Four points may be made with regard to their daily wage:

1. Daily wage differs from region to region within CN area.

2. There is gross disparity in the wage men receive and women receive as coolies.

3. During dry spells of the year when there are no agriculture activity daily wage touches bottom line.

4. No monetary aid or relief is given in case of fatal accident or death. Highly insecure occupations.

The following table indicates the daily wage of men and women coolies in different villages:

	Male	Female	Villages
1.	Rs.500/	Rs.150/	Kastur, Madapura, Hadya.
2.	Rs.400/	Rs.150/	Bhogapura
3.	Rs.300/	Rs.150/, 120/	M.Hosur, Bedarapura, Kellamballi, etc,
4.	Rs.250/	Rs.100/	Maskapura, Talawadi, etc,
5.	Rs.200/	Rs.120/	Tignare,etc

The above table is self explanatory pointing to, among other things, 1) the low daily wage of agriculture coolies and 2) the prevailing gender inequality in wage and variations in wage from season to season.

Landholding among Christian respondents

Nearly 1/3 of Christian families are landless

It should be noted that Christians are not altogether landless people but own some lands of their own, in most villages. As per the Sample survey as many as 72.5% of all Christian families own a piece of land. However this fact is not a matter to be cheered up much for two reasons:

- Firstly, most of the pieces of land Christians own are **dry** land which means cultivation is totally dependent on unpredictable rainfall.

- Secondly, most of the landholding of Christian families are very small pieces, average size being 1-2 acres only.

Landholding among Christian families in CN area:
Sample families – total- 360

I.	Landless families	28 % (101 families)
II.	Families having land	72% (259 families)

Only 19% among the land owning families own 'wet' land all the rest own only 'dry' land

Total land owning families - 269

I.	those owning **wet** land	19%
II.	Those owning **dry** land	81%

The above statistics from the Sample survey are self –explanatory indicating, by and large, the landless/landholding condition of Christian community. Further the survey has discovered that in as many as 12 villages, out of 26 villages surveyed, no wet land was owned by Christian families, at all. All of them owned small pieces of dry land only, cultivation of which was dependant totally on highly erratic rain fall. On the other hand in about six villages especially Kastur and Kellamballi a good number of Christian families found to own wet land. Needless to say that the wet land ownership meant relatively a better economic condition. **Meager size of land holdings—as high as 80% among those own land possess only small patch of land of the size between 1/4 acre to 3 acres.**

The land owned by Christians was not only mostly dry one but also very small in size. The following statistics are self explanatory:

Among those owned land (72% owned land):

- As high as 80% owned land of the size of ¼ acres to 3 acres.

- Among those who owned land:

- As few as only 20% owned land of the size 4 acres and above, however most of such land did not cross more than 6 acres.

Majority Christian families own hardly any other assets of any value

It is very difficult to expect ownership of assets worth mentioning from a community which lives in hand to mouth condition. The meager and poor quality of land holding pattern found with Christians actually mirrors the community's very poor economic condition.

Interesting responses were received from the respondents to queries on whether their family owns some specific gadgets or home essentials.

A good majority of families own mobile phone, T.V. and cooking gas

According to the data received 2-3 items were owned by most/ larger number of Christian families. These items were:

Firstly, mobile phone owned by	89%
Secondly, TV owned by	82%
Thirdly, cooking gas	64%

Interestingly, two gadgets, mobile phone and T.V. have become very essentials of life today, even in as rural as CN area. Yet another much aspired devise was cooking gas. Our Sample study found that as many as 64% of all Christian families in CN area have now switched to cooking gas, giving up the traditional and health hazardous firewood cooking. Needless to say this is a welcome development particularly in view of family health, especially of women folk.

Christians own barely minimal agricultural essentials/ implements, live stock etc.

It was discovered that only 19% of Christian families rear livestock, in small numbers (cow, sheep, goat and poultry). For a community which is still largely dependent on agriculture the fact that only a small 19% rear livestock is too minimal. In fact it was discovered that in 9 villages out of 26 villages of the Sample survey none of the Christian families owned any livestock. There may be two possible reasons for this situation: first, the poor economic condition of Christians which does not allow them to buy / invest in livestock. Second, lack of sufficient interest or motivation to venture in dairy or other livestock which could be potentially good income generating.

Among Christian families very few owned pump set. Only 23 families (out of 360 families) owned pump sets. Bullock carts and tractors which are essential for agriculture are still very meagerly owned by Christians. So also the case of bore wells. It was discovered that only 16 families owned bore well.

Heavy burden of debt

It is part of history of CN Christian community how their fore fathers/mothers had suffered horrendous consequences of debt trap, just a hundred years ago. In those days the local land lord was the main money lender for the village poor. One of the serious consequences of debt trap was bonded labour (jitha) or slavery. When people were unable to pay back the borrowed amount and its interest, not only adult men and women were subjected to slavery but even children of very tender age were pushed into lifelong slavery. It was George William Sawday the pioneer Missionary, who struggled for many years in CN villages and redeemed scores of people in slavery, especially the tender aged slave children assuring them new lease of life.

In independent India jitha is banned by the law of the land. Though legally banned there is every good reason to believe that the oppressive jitha practice is still alive in remote villages.

Today, though bonded labour is disappearing, due to the persisting poor economic condition a great majority of CN Christians are under the yoke of debt trap. In a situation where people had to constantly require money for survival, life becomes an endless struggle. Be it for the repair of their falling fragile houses/ huts, for emergencies like serious sickness, children's education, marriage of children as well as to expenses related to agricultural work they all are in dire need of money, all the time.

Our Sample survey brought out the fact that among 200 respondents who reported that they were in debt, 39% stated they had borrowed for the purpose of house repair/re-construction or even for a construction of a new house. Nineteen percent stated that they had to borrow for cultivation purpose. Ten percent stated that they borrowed for children's education. While a little lesser percentage of families had borrowed money for buying livestock, for marriage or in a difficult time.

Decades ago land lord/money lender was the main source to borrow money. The money lender belonged to upper/dominant caste and they played havoc with lives of hapless poor borrowers. Exorbitant compound interest, fraud, cheating, extortion, violence and slavery, in that vicious order the money lending business of the time operated.

Hold of traditional village money lenders has weakened— but Banks are inaccessible to poor and illiterates

It's a welcome sign that the role of traditional money lender has weakened quite considerably, today. The government intends to help out the village poor through banks and other financial institutions. However as on today the banking sector is still one which is not easily approachable as far as the poor people are concerned. Many CN Christians expressed this concern very much. Adding to it in many villages Christian families reported how the government and the bank officials show a prejudiced mind and harass Christian applicants when they approach for loans.

Self Help Groups (SHGs), NGOs –a beacon of hope

It is at this context the formation of Self Help Groups (SHGs), women Sanghas, Milk Federation, Rudset (Dharmastala temple initiative) and other societies are proving to be a boon to the village poor, including Christians. Following statistics point out this fact clearly:

1. Among Christians families who borrowed those borrowed from SHGs , Sanghas,NGOs   50%
2. From Banks   33%
3. From money lenders   17%

The above table is self explanatory. It points out how SHGs and women Sanghas are catching up and helping people in need. It's a welcome sign that the network of SHGs and women associations are found in many of the villages where the present Sample survey was under taken.

Self-assessment on economic condition – Majority of Christians greatly disillusioned

To a question on the general economic condition only 1/3 of the total respondent families expressed some satisfaction stating that there was some good economic progress taking place. The rest of 2/3 of the families were however unequivocal in stating that the economic condition remained stagnant (40%) and as many as 23% pointing out that it was totally deplorable, turning from bad to worse.

True, the economic condition in general turning from bad to worse was the cry of most of Christians. Out of the 26 villages surveyed as many as 11 villages either totally or overwhelmingly registered that the economic condition was in a very bad shape.

The data collected clearly exposes the darker side of the professed 'development' and that a real progress of people had not yet reached the poor.

Christians and State Reservation

Very few among Christians avail state benefits—lack of awareness, lack of organized efforts and communal prejudice main causes

As it is known that Central and the State governments have innumerable provisions and schemes which intend to bring the historically under privileged sections of the population in par with the others. Among the listed under privileged communities include mainly scheduled castes (SC/Dalit), Scheduled tribes (ST/Adivasi) and also religious minorities, women and others.

Among the Central and State reservations include, mainly:

1. **Scheduled Caste (SC) reservation:** This is mainly given to people who were historically suppressed as 'untouchables'. SC provisions of reservation covers a very wide range of educational, employment, economic, political reservations and civil rights with innumerable projects, schemes, grants to uplift Scheduled Caste people. The Government of India has granted this reservation provision to "Hindu" Dalits, and later also to Dalits in Sikh and Buddhist religions. However until now the Indian government has not granted SC reservation to Christians coming from the same social origin.

2. The granting of Scheduled Caste reservation solely rests with the Government of India or the Central Government.

3. **OBC reservation:** A number of states in India have granted certain reservation provisions to backward caste people other than SCs and STs. Karnataka State Government also has set up a Commission for OBC and has granted several reservation provisions to people of backward communities, irrespective of religion. Accordingly in Karnataka state Christians of depressed class origin come under Category – I of OBC reservation and entitled for benefits, mainly educational, employment and so on. However most Christians of depressed class origin in Karnataka fail to avail these provisions either due to lack of awareness on their part/ in the community and or due to apathy of church leadership. The harassment they face by the communally prejudiced government officials was reportedly yet another serious obstacle.

4. **Religious minorities benefits:** Karnataka State has a Minority Commission and a Minority Development Corporation. Through these institutions the State government intends to

give a special support to religious minorities such as Muslims, Christians, Jains and Buddhists. The minority provisions include mainly educational and economical, empowering projects through soft loans and financial support. Again due to lack of awareness about the beneficial schemes and provisions Christian families could seldom make use of the minority provisions at all.

Our Sample survey brought out few important facts as related to reservations /state benefits:

1. It was found that only a small segment, as small as 1/5th of Christian families availed some governmental provisions meant for weaker sections and minorities.

2. Lack of awareness in the Christian community was a major problem in the Christian community. Even the pastors/ church leaders do not appear to be having a proper knowledge about any of the state reservation provision. The church leadership appears to be very apathic/indifferent about the whole matter.

3. Few villages in CN area like Kastur, Madapura, Maskapura, Kellamballi, M.Hosur, etc., made use of some government benefits, relatively better. But in most villages families were almost fully ignorant of them. In eight villages out of 26, none of the Christian families were aware of any governmental reservations/benefits, at all. The Christian families in Talwadi region availed some benefits from the government but they reported that they had to face much harassment and religious prejudice from the officials.

4. Among those availed state benefits most got them on account of house repair or for construction of a new house. Other provisions they received, though very minimal, included

widow's pension, old age pension, soft loan for agricultural or educational purpose and toilet constructions.

5. Repeated plea of people to disseminate important 'info' on State provisions.

6. It was very striking that a large number of respondents repeatedly pleaded that the church leadership should take lead in passing on or updating them with vital information on all important/new schemes for weaker sections and minorities etc. They believed that such an initiative from the church will create awareness among people and thus help much in empowering Christian community.

Christians and politics

The Wesleyan missionaries generally carried quite some reservations on Indian national freedom, freedom movement and Congress Party. It was also true that many freedom fighters/Congress men were active in anti-Christian/missionary agitations during missionaries' time, i.e. in 1920s and 1930s.

Understandably the Christian congregations carry considerable impact of those historical developments. After Independence, Christians by and large resorted to be pro- Congress supporters. This trend continues to be the case until now.

On the basis of the findings of the survey following few points may be made:

–   Christians are generally regular voters in all elections.

–   The political awareness has considerably increased among Christians in recent years.

– However not many Christians were found as members of elected local bodies. Out of 26 villages surveyed,in only five villages a Christian village Panchayat member was found. The number of Christians in political parties as members was just bare minimum.

– There is a dire need of imparting social-political education to Christians so that they can more actively and meaningfully participate in political process.

Unabated migration—and it is escalating

In about 50% of Christian families as many as 1-3 members migrated to other places

Migration is a universal phenomenon. It is not new to people of CN area either. In fact migration of people is very much part of CN history, from time unknown.

In modern time the migration continued unabated, rapidly and unending. Erratic rain fall, uncertainty of cultivation or unproductive agriculture, lack of industries, unemployment have all aggravated migration process at a very rapid phase, year after year, in CN area.

The Sample survey has discovered that among all Christian families in CN area in 47% families 1-3 members of a family had migrated to other places. While in some villages migration appear to be very extensive, in a few villages migration is relatively less. In most of the villages in CN area respondents lamented that all their able bodied have left the villages, as a result of which the local church/community has become almost 'lifeless'.

Village congregations have become 'life less' due to ongoing migration

When one observes the alarming number of aged and disabled couples living all alone in most CN villages the stark reality of endless migration opens up itself. During the course of field study in several villages Christians bemoaned how their community had become 'life less', lacked luster because of the large scale migration from village. Migration had stunted the very growth of the church and community lamented many people, passionately, in Kerehalli, Heggevadi, Mudnakod and several other villages.

Bengaluru—Most favorite destination of migration

A century ago CN migrants used to migrate to Nilgiris, Wayanad, Coorg, and even to Ceylon to work in coffee or tea estates. However after the dawn of an industrial era in India and the beginning of construction of dams and reservoirs people started migrating to those places in larger number. However for the last 4-5 decades the state capital Bengaluru has become the hot destination of most of the CN migrants. In fact this city has become the favored destination for people from all places, far beyond the state.

While the hostile geo-social-economic problems 'push' villagers out, Bengaluru with bountiful labour opportunities is 'pulling' them all, in.

According to our Sample survey of all the CN migrants,

> 42% migrated to Bengaluru
> 26% to Mysore city
> 32% to scores of other places

Other destinations of migrants

As indicated in the table above 32% of all those CN migrants went to places other than Bengaluru and Mysore. Which are those other places? If some of those places were within CN district, few others were in different parts of Karnataka, Some even outside Karnataka including few handfuls in Middle East countries.

Within the district people migrated, for example, to CN town, the district headquarters, and to places like Madapura, Talwadi. Within the states quite a number of CN migrants moved to Tumkur, Hassan, Mangalore, Chikamagalur, Hunsur, and so on. Outside the state included Coimbatore, Gopi in Tamilnadu. Quite a few from Kirugunda and Hadya villages moved to Nanjanagudu the famous temple town adjacent to Chamarajanagara district.

It is interesting that a handful family reported that 1 or 2 of their family members were settled in Saudi-Arabia, Kuwait, Dubai and so on.

Occupations of migrant members—No significant upward occupational mobility

The Sample survey pointed out that a larger number of CN migrants to Bengaluru, Mysore and other places are engaged in skilled or unskilled jobs such as factory hand, electrician, painter, mason, carpenter, mechanic, driver and so on. Some others worked as security staff or watchman or peon in industrial units, schools, offices and church establishments. Quite a number of CN migrants worked as coolies or unskilled labourers for their livelihood. It is very striking that their occupational pattern appeared almost as a replica of what they/their people were doing in CN villages, except of course the agricultural occupation. A second line of occupation in which quite a few migrants found were as office clerk, teacher, basic computer worker, nurse/paramedical, lab technician, pastor and so on. A handful even venture in to petty real estate business.

As far as professionals were concerned very few among migrants/ or in their family found as engineer, doctor, officer, lecturer and so on.

Among women migrants most of them found as nurse, teacher, lab technician, garment worker, office clerk, peon, coolie, house maid and so on.

The findings re-iterate the fact that the CN migrants have not achieved any noticeable upward occupational mobility after migrating to other places/cities. As noted earlier their occupational pattern continued as a replica or a continuum of what they were doing in their villages.

Caste factor

Root cause behind many lingering problems of Christians

It is an undeniable fact that in spite of professed goal of democracy and secular state caste continues to be at the back of most of the persisting problems of Indian society.

The CN village Christians, all from depressed class social origin, unable to bear the untold caste oppression any more had embraced Christian faith during the first half of last century. They had an earnest hope that the new faith would assure them a life of justice, freedom and dignity. There was a great backlash against them when they made the decision to embrace Christian faith. They faced the backlash boldly. The neo converts faced all trials and tribulation because they carried a great and in-explicable sense of meaning and solace in their new found faith. The new community nurtured in Christian faith and grew as a community, largely free from caste/ practices in the midst of a caste ruled society.

Christians continued to be 'looked down' as inferior

However, despite their conversion to a new faith the caste Hindu community/village community continues to 'look down' and treat them as inferior people. Christians had to suffer much caste humiliation with a grin. True, there were also occasions when Christians stood up united and resisted caste oppression on them, when humiliation on them crossed certain limit.

Today, due to many socio-political compulsions and the changed dynamics direct or open caste violence against depressed class people,Christians has been noticeably reduced. However following points in the light of the findings of Sample survey may be noted:

1. Verbal caste abuses are still made on Christians on many occasions. Christians particularly educated younger generation, are deeply hurt about it. However, since they do not see a way out, they try to ignore them as common occurrence. Only when verbal abuse becomes too aggressive Christians tend to resist and the conflict usually ends as a skirmish.

2. Despite an inferior mindset about Christians still lingering it must be however noted that more and more caste Hindus mingle quite well with Christians in villages, in day to day interactions. In most of the villages Christians vouched that people were all cordial and they all live well, together. The 'standard' response of most Christians would be: 'we are all together. No one is discriminated because of caste'.

3. Only a deeper probe could bring out actual and painful reality on how caste was still operative and a problem.

4.   Our Sample survey affirmed the fact that by and large Christians have no issues with backward caste people, at all. After all most of them too like Christians live in a condition of poverty.

5.   The respondents in many villages repeatedly informed that Lingayats, of all the communities, carry maximum contempt on Christians and often openly show their repulsion. Generally, Lingayats hardly have any social interaction with Christians, in CN villages.

Christians and 'Hindu' Dalits – there exists unity as well as conflict among them

In most villages "Hindu" Dalits are good compatriots of Christians because of their homogenous social origin as well as common suffering. In villages like Heggewadi a very cordial relationship and co-existence was reported. So also in a number of other places.

However some serious problems between those two opressed communities were also discovered. In Kellamballi, Kirugunda and Hadya villages Christians were reportedly harassed none other than by 'Hindu' Dalits. In village like Hadya small scuffles or conflicts between 'Hindu' Dalit youth and Christian youth take place. Such cases which were disturbing peace and harmony.

There were occasions in village life when Christians and Dalits were directly or indirectly humiliated on account of their 'inferior' social origin. A regular occasion in which humiliation was shown on them was while drawing water from village well during dry spell. Further many respondents reported that they often suffer caste humiliation on account of their conversion to a 'foreign' faith while applying for a governmental benefit in village panchayat office or revenue offices. This was reported generally in most villages, however, more intensively in Talwadi region of CN area.

Do Christians 'look down' at Dalits?

During the field study, few respondents found gleefully claiming that they neither go to Dalit locality nor do they mingle with them. In a way that reflected the upper caste attitude towards Dalits. Do Christians unconsciously develop a feeling that they now belonged to a higher religion/caste? Further study is needed before drawing any conclusion.

The need to orient Christians in liberative and inclusive Christian faith as well as stressing the need of standing in solidarity with all the marginalized is very urgent.

Caste and church property disputes

Casteist violence against Christians was quite often manifested as related to church property also. In quite a few CN village like M.Hosur the contempt of caste Hindus against Christians was expressed through baseless charges and creating disputes on church property matters to harass a vulnerable local Christian community.

Due to this, Christians in Kellamballi had to face unnecessary problems while they were constructing a new church building. In M. Hosur, villagers did not allow Christians to build a compound wall to Mission hospital, till date. Justifying their opposition, village leaders say, 'If you build a compound wall tomorrow you will construct a church.'

Christian women

Women-prime spiritual nurturers

Women in CN village congregations are undoubtedly the prime nurturers of families and congregations, including spiritual life.

Though those women were simple rural folk of meager economic resource and of very little or no education they keep the light kindled and strives to keep it burning, which is amazing. Thanks for the strong foundation laid during initial decades of founding of those congregations through a well organized and vigilant pastoral care and Christian nurture.

It was found that it was generally women who attend the worship services, in larger number. Further it was always women in more number who partake in communion, more than men folk. Even in Christian Giving generally women folk are setting an example in spite their meager economic condition.

Women's critical-constructive participants

It was discovered that when they were asked to comment on the present state of the church/Christian community, women were exceptionally forthright in criticizing the lapses of pastors and diocesan leadership, directly and sparing none. Their critique was found to be practical, balanced and objective and was aimed only in the best interest of the community and the church. Their understanding of the church and their vision of the church growth were also incisive which makes them truly critical participants in the life and growth of the church.

Greater concern for education among women

Thanks again for the educational work of Wesleyan Mission especially among women. If today a good majority of Christians in CN villages are literate and many were quite educated too to their class, and if there is a growing motivation for education the credit goes to Wesleyan Mission legacy and the pivotal role played by women. Scores of CN village girls were sent and admitted to girl boarding homes and schools in Mysore and Hassan etc, where they were not only educated but also thoroughly groomed in Christian womanhood. When they returned to their families in their villages they brought them a positive, nay, a catalytic impact which was enormous especially in upbringing children and family imparting spiritual nurture. They became an asset in the growth of the local congregations.

Growing number of post graduate girls in CN villages

It is not surprising that today girls out beat boys in schooling. Even in number of graduates and post graduates girls are now giving a tough competition to boys. As per our Sample survey following number of male and female graduates and post graduates were found in CN villages:

Number of graduate and post graduate level persons among respondent families (total families-360)

		Male	Female	Total
1.	Graduate level	45	36	81
2.	Post-graduate level	10	11	21

Challenges which Christian women face in CN Area:

Gender inequality continued

Although women play an important role in upbringing of families by and large gender inequality against them continues, directly or indirectly. Similarly there are also cases reported of gender violence or domestic cruelties against women in congregations.

Although women are the prime spiritual nurturers and back bone of the church/community and its growth, they are hardly found in church leadership, in pastorate committees or as pastors or Bible Women, During Wesleyan Mission period at times there were four Bible Women actively working in the planting and growth of the church in CN area. But today there is not even a single

Bible Woman or somebody working exclusively amongst women.

A large number of women unemployed or under employed

There are a remarkable number of women between the age group of 20-40 in CN area who are metric, post metric or even graduate but most of those women were discovered to be unemployed or underemployed. If appropriate trade/skill training is given to them they could become a great source of empowerment to their families and to the community.

It is a striking fact that this situation is well realized by Christian community including women. One repeated plea of village Christians was to impart job-oriented training to women, on an urgent and priority basis, which could empower the families.

Religious Condition

Sixteen pastorates in CN area

The congregations in CN Area are presently part of sixteen pastorates. Some of the pastorates have 1-2 substations. The largest among the pastorates include, Kastur and Madapura.

Following is the list of Pastorates in CN district:

Pastorates (Sub-stations are noted within brackets)

1. C.N Town (Nagavalli)
2. Kastur (Homma, Ankusharayanapura)
3. M. Hosur (Deshavalli, Basavatti)
4. Bhogapura (Kiragsur)
5. Madapura (Andrakalli, Doddarayana Pet)
9. Heggewadi (Kerehalli, Mudnakod)
10. Kollegala (Bluff)
11. Talwadi (T. Hosur)
12. Dodda Gajanur
13. Tiganare (Karlavadi)

6. Masgapura   14. Singonapura (Malakalli)
7. Kellamballi   15. Metluvadi
8. Bedarapura   16. Ugani

Note: Hadya and Kirugunda are not in the above list, since they are part of Mysore Area.

Church institutions, schools, hospitals etc., then and now.
During the Wesleyan Mission period (Pre-independence time) there were following Mission institutions in CN area:

THEN

Schools – 9 (in 1940s)
Hospitals – 2 (Kastur and Hadya)
Weekly clinics – about 2-3 (including M Hosur, CN Town)
Ashram/Women's resource centre – 2 (Kastur and Hadya)
Leprosy eradiation work – in villages of Talwadi region
Bible Women – maximum 4 in 1930s and 40s

NOW (as on end of 2016)

Schools – 2 (Kastur, C.N Town)
Hospital – 1 (M.Hosur)
Clinics – Nil
Ashram – Nil
Day Care centres – 2 (M. Hosur, T. Hosur)
Bible Women – Nil

Spiritual nurture activities
Sunday Service, Wednesday worship, cottage prayer meeting, Youth fellowship, Women's fellowship, Sunday school and Temperance meetings were once very regular and active programmes in the

CN congregations. They helped in the spiritual nurture of the Christian Community and in the growth of the church.

However the above noted spiritual activities are not found in many congregations. Only in a few congregations like Kastur and Kellamballi, Sunday School, Youth Fellowship, and Women's fellowship and such other activities were found to some extent.

C.N area continues to contribute presbyters

It goes to the credit of CN area that from the time of the Wesleyan Mission until now many young men and even a few women have come forward to enter theological seminary and have become pastors. Kastur, M.Hosur and Bhogapura are three villages which made maximum contribution in this regard. This good legacy continues even now and a number of presbyters presently serving Karnataka Southern Diocese and to some extent even Karnataka Central Diocese, hail from CN Area.

One striking fact is that for a long time, pastors of Basel Mission back ground from coastal region used to go to CN area including Mysore area and serve the churches there as pastors, in considerable number. However, presently it is reverse; a good number of presbyters from CN area are now serving as pastors in former Basel Mission area of Mangalore, Udupi and Coorg.

Two important grievances/appeals of Christian community in CN area:

Two prominent appeals or grievances were very vocal in CN congregations. They are:

1. The need of residential Pastors

In many villages people appealed repeatedly and passionately that they need a pastor who would reside in their midst and help in their spiritual nurture and also in their social empowerment. The repeated outcry of the people was that the pastors are not often around, when they were really in dire need. In fact, in quite a few village congregations it was complained that the pastors reside with their families in distant town or city and come only to their village for Sunday worship for an hour or two and return. It was discovered that out 16 pastorates in CN area only four had residential pastors, two had residential deacons, one had a non-ordained church worker and the rest of nine pastorates had no residential pastors at all. There is an urgent need on the part of of the church leadership to look into this grave situation, without further delay.

2. Passionate appeal to the Diocese to provide help to children's education and for other needs.

Motivation for education even for higher education is fast growing among Christians in CN villages. However, their economic condition does not allow them to pursue education, especially college education. In the course of the Sample survey it was a very common out cry of people that the Diocese should help in their children's education on a regular basis and even for college education. Many also appealed that their below poverty condition demands that the church should help them in improving their lot, including housing and agriculture activities.

Added many village Christians appealed that in a context were women were either unemployed/under employed, proper vocational training provided to them by the Diocese, on an urgent basis.

Concluding summary

General

Christians in CN villages are part of the poorer section of the population. Their habitat, housing, resources all reflect the difficult socio-economic condition in which they live.

Christian families are mostly nuclear and small in size.

Christian families are mostly nuclear families where husband, wife and children live under one roof. The number of joint families is almost fully declining, year after year.

Over the passing of time Christian families have also become small in size. On an average the family has two children.

Majority of Christian families own land but they are small and dry ones.

About 3/4th of all Christian families in CN area own land, however most of them are small patches of land and dry land. This means their land is unable to sustain them.

More than 50% of working force work as agriculture coolies; increasing number go for non-agriculture jobs.

Little over 50% of all adult Christian men or women toil as agricultural coolies, mostly in the lands of village land lords. True, many of those families own land but they are small and dry lands unable to sustain them economically.

The daily wage is minimal and varies region to region.

An agricultural coolie gets about Rs.500/ per day in a few villages, however in most villages he/she gets only about Rs. 300/ or Rs. 200/. In the present context where the cost of living, cost of essentials including housing, medicare, education and so on have become very exorbitant, the pittance of daily wage is hardly sufficient to support the families.

Traditional money lenders are losing hold. However Christians are big debtors. Self Help Groups proving to be helpful to people.

Christians borrow for their various needs. While banks and such other financial institutions are largely inaccessible to them and the mass, the Self-Help Groups and NGOs are proving to be a boon to people.

Christians are largely literates but post-metric/college education is minimal. Professional education is very rare.

A majority of Christian is literate, but most of them end up at metric or under metric level due to poverty. Motivation for education including for college education is greatly rising but most Christian families cannot afford it.

Christians are greatly disillusioned with economic policies/programmes of government.

Majority of Christians feel that the Governmental economic programmes are totally deplorable since they hardly reach them.

A great lack of awareness on Governmental benefits and reservations.

Christians admitted that there is a great lack of awareness among Christians about various governmental provisions meant to weaker sections and minorities. Therefore they were unable to avail those provisions. It was also reported that they have none to guide them in this matter.

Communal prejudice/harassment plays a big role in depriving Christians from availing state benefits

Christians are often twice harassed: firstly, because of their depressed class social origin, secondly, because they have embraced a different (Christian) religion.

Rapid / growing migration and its many negative impacts.

Christian community, like all other poor communities in CN area suffers from negative impacts of migration. Migration has made village congregations almost lifeless. Further when all the able-bodied men with their families left the villages the aged, disabled and widows left in lurch in villages. The large number of widows and aged couples living all alone is a matter of grave concern.

Caste/casteism does not allow Christians to live with dignity and freedom.

Direct/open caste violence on Christians is greatly reduced now. Christians and caste Hindus (especially OBCs) increasingly intermingle. However, by and large, still Christians are 'looked down' for their alleged low social origin. Although verbal caste abuse is quite reduced it is still prevalent. Christians, especially youth suffer the humiliations, bitterly and painfully.

Christians are regular voters.

Christians vote regularly in elections. Their awareness in politics has considerably increased. However, they are not found very much as members of political parties or as members of village council (panchayat). Imparting of a proper political education to Christian community is very much needed.

Women are mostly unemployed or under employed.

There is an urgent need to impart vocational /trade training to women, which could empower the community considerably.

Gender inequality prevails. Positively, increasing number of girls pursue education and competing well with boys.

Gender inequality, in various forms including domestic violence prevails in the community. Women are chief spiritual nurturers and in many cases even bread winners in the families, but they have little or no voice in decision making, even in the congregations.

Women are prime spiritual nurturers.

Women are prime spiritual nurturers in families and in the congregations. They are also remarkably forthright, critical and constructive critics of pastors and church leaders, often in the best interest of the community/ church.

Majority of people feel that pastoral care/work is very much neglected/collapsed.

People report that the pastoral care/work is not the same what it used to be. It was a common outcry among people that they need only those pastors who would live in their midst, help in their spiritual nurture as well as in their social empowerment.

An intense pastoral care along with implementation of an effective and integrated socio-economic empowerment programme, implemented in a priority basis could go a long way in rejuvenating the congregations in CN area.

References

I. Primary Source

- MDR (Mysore District Report-(Annual Reports of Wesleyan Mission) Years: 1848 to 1861, 1874-1947

- Register of Adult Baptisms of WM Mission in CN area.

- Harvest Field. Years: 1907-1910, 1914-1919, 1921-1927.

- NCCI Review. Years: 1928-1927, 1939-1948.

- Bodhaka Bhodini. Years: 1911, 1937-1940.

- Arthur, William, *Mission to Mysore*, 1850, London

- Thompson E.W, *The Call of India*, WMMS, London, 1912.

- Findley, G. G. and Holdsworth, W.W, *The History of WMMS*, Volume V, London, 1924.

- Statement of Mysore District Policy-Wesleyan Mission, 1936.

- WMMS Provincial Committee Report- 1938.

- WMMS in Ceylon, India, Burma-Report of Secretary William Goudie, London, 1936.

- The Methodist Church Overseas Mission Report of 1936-1937, Bishopsgate, London, 1937.

- Methodist Church in South India, Report of the Commission to the Mysore District, 1941.

II. Other References

- Sargant, *N C and Ward, A. M,* 'W.E. Tomlinson', CLS, Madras, 1952.

- Sargant, *N C - From Missions to Church in Karnataka*, CLS, Madras, 1987.

- Sargant, *N C - Origin of the Christian Church in Mysore State*, ICH Review, May 1962.

- Soans C. - *Development of Leadership in the Kannada speaking Churches of WM Mission in Karnataka*, M.Th thesis, U.T.College, 1984.

- Vijaya Kumar, *Educational Policy of WMMS in Mysore*, M.Th Thesis, U.T.College, Bangalore.

- Devadas, Charles, Late Rev. George William Sawday, unpublished.

- Vijayakumar, *The Wesleyan Methodist Mission and Missionaries*, unpublished, 2011.

- Prabhu, Franklin. Rev. George William Sawday: 1854-1944, not dated, unpublished.

- Giriraj, *Founding of Churches and their Growth in CN Area.* (In Kannada) B.D.thesis. KTC, 1985.

- Shashi Kumar, *Pastoral Work in CSI Churches in Chamarajanagara and Socio-economic Religious condition (in Kannada)*, B.D. thesis, KTC, 1995.

- Wilson H.S, *Wesleyan Kanarese Mission in the Mysore Territory*, ICH review, June 1986.

III. Sample Survey

– Sample Survey conducted in 26 villages of CN area.

– Date: from 20 to 30ᵗʰ October, 2016.

– Presbyters and Lay Leaders interviewed:

– Prof. Samson Dixit (Madapura/Bangalore), Rev. Dr. Charles Devadas(Bhogapura/Bangalore), Prasanna(Kastur), Rev. Puttaraju (Madapura), Rev. Shashikumar (Hadya), Rev. Hemachandra, (Kastur), Rev. S,C. Babu (Kollegala), Rev. Stephen Aravind(Talwadi) Mr. Jaison Gouder(Mettluwadi), Rev. Thyagaraj, (Masgapura/CN town), Rev. Mrs. Usha Thyagaraj (CN Town), Prof. Samson Sadhu, (Mysore), Dr. D. Yohana (Mysore), Rev. P. Gurushantha (Mysore), Rev. Sister Sujatha (Mysore), Mr.D. Sachidananda(Mysore).

By the Same Author

Christian Social concern books

- *Plight of Christian Dalits- A South Indian Case Study,* ATC, Bangalore, 1997.

- *Kannada version (concise) of Plight of Christian Dalits, "Dalitha Kraistharu",* CISRS, Bangalore, 1997; reprinted in 1998.

- *Our Slums: Mirror a Systemic Malady, A study of Bangalore slums,* ATC, Bangalore 1999.

- *Dalit Christians – A Saga of Faith and Pathos,* ISPCK, New Delhi & NCCI, Nagpur, 2012.

- *A Hand Book for Socio-economic Empowerment of Christians,* CSI Karnataka Inter-diocesan Literature Board, Bangalore, 2013.

- *Christian Dalit Women, A South Indian Case Study,* ISPCK, New-Delhi, 2015.

Rev. G.W. Sawday

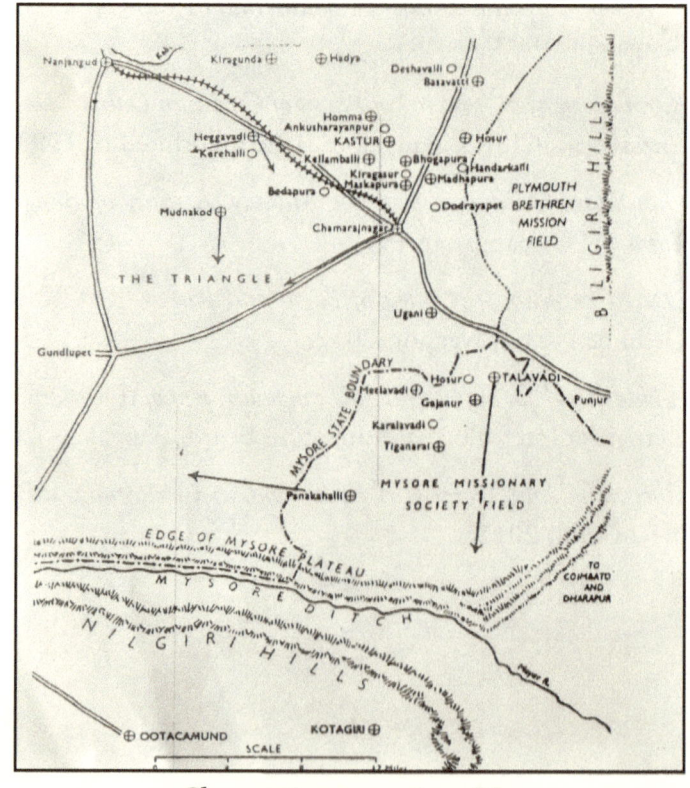

Chamarajanagara Area Map

www.ingramcontent.com/pod-product-compliance
Lightning Source LLC
Chambersburg PA
CBHW030406020726
47493CB00003B/969